WHAT I DO IS

TABOO...3

Published by
PF and Associates

ISBN-13: 978-0-9769772-2-3

Interior Designed by The Writer's Assistant.com

WHAT I DO IS

TABOO...3

Yonder

What I Do Is Taboo

Your clit is what I am after
I take care of it so well
You become my personal freak
That's why what I do is Taboo

Intense orgasms are promised
Impulsive sex is what I offer
Toes at attention and a permanent smile
Is what you will have
That's why what I do is Taboo

Sex with me is for the adventurous
'Cause it's seldom done in the bedroom
Let's start on the pool table
And end in the pool
From this moment on
Consider yourself addicted to me
That's really why what I do is Taboo

The Chronicles of Lance
by T.L. Rawlings

In Love with a Stripper
(Based on a True Story)

"She had the body of a goddess..."

That was obvious. See, she believed in physical fitness to the utmost. This was not a game. Her body was one of God's great creations.

And, like an artist's apprentice, she took hold of her sculpted structure and enhanced it to perfection.

The first time we met, I was only sixteen. I had no business in her domain. Though I was a master of covert operations, able to lie about my age and act ten years my elder, so when I looked at her, I realized I wasn't ready.

As the bartender tapped my Heineken bottle, I put $6.00 on the bar and, even though I was intimidated, I could not stop making eye contact with her. Our glare became so deep the other patrons were looking at me.

One of the regulars blurted out, "Who the fuck..."

She sashayed over to me, moved my Heineken, looked me in my eyes, smiled, put both her hands on my head, and introduced me to the most glorious breasts I've ever tasted. As she flexed her pectoral muscles, her titties massaged my head like a machine.

The whole place erupted like a Chicago Bulls game. Mike must have scored! As she raised my head, it was as if I had just taken a toke of a freshly rolled 1975 joint... straight Reefer...intimidation right out the window. We looked into each other's eyes. Then she pulled my ear close to her lips and whispered, "Wait for me..."

Two in the morning seemed to come as fast as an excited teenager at a basement party. As my boys and I left the spot, my man Vince asked, "Yo...what did she say?"

"Wait for me," I said.

"Oooohh shit! You lucky motherfucker. I guess I'll holla at you later. Damn!"

"Yeah, later yo," I said, still thinking this was a dream sequence from *Weird Science* or some John Cusack movie.

At about 2:20 AM she came out of the club. Before I could wave to her, a dude carrying two bags followed her out to her car across the street.

"Damn..." Kind of relieved, I glanced over to watch them leave.

When they got to the car, I could tell they weren't together. His "gentleman act" was his way of trying to get her number.

I started laughing and walking away when...

"EXCUSE ME...SO YOU'RE LEAVING?!"

I looked over my shoulder and she was staring me dead in my face. Booyow...got ya nigga, as Hulk Hogan would say, "WHATCHAGONNA DOOO?"

"I thought you had company. I was gonna roll," I explained, walking across the street toward her.

"If you didn't want to go with me all you had to say was no."

"Nah...it wasn't like that...I just..."

"Get in," she ordered. Damn!

I didn't have enough time to be scared. It was like Jodeci, "Don't talk...just listen."

Her car smelled almost as good as she did. It smelled sexy. Was that possible? I later found out that it was Sun, Moon, & Stars, a fragrance that many dancers loved. If a girl was clean before she put it on, it was the shit!

"What's your name, sexy?" she asked

"Lance. What's yours?"

"Dream," she said, as she maneuvered her hand from the stick shift to mine.

Dream was the perfect name. I knew going in that she was never going to leave my mind.

"I'm hungry as hell...you hungry?" she asked.

"Girl, food is the last thing on my mind!"

We busted out laughing as she hopped on the beltway.

"Yeah, I am kinda hungry. Where were you going?" I asked.

"Going? Man I have a fridge full of food. I can cook my damn self."

"I'm sorry...we'll see...cooking huh...stop playing," I said partially impressed.

As we talked, it seemed as if there was no reason to be fearful. She was cool peeps. It just so happened that she had a body I would pay to be with, and I don't believe in paying for booty, at least not directly anyway.

Dream was a master conversationalist, so much so that when she pulled into her garage, I had no clue where we were. I just knew we left downtown Baltimore at 2:30AM and it was now 3:00AM.

The crib was serious! The garage was the size of a small apartment, with an Astroturf floor, and air-conditioned. A spiral staircase led into the house.

"Are you scared of dogs?" she asked.

"Nope, just teeth," I said.

"You are crazy!" she blurted as she smiled.

When we reached the top of the stairs, she pressed an intercom and said something in another language.

"My dog's trainer gives him commands in Japanese so only a couple of people know how to control him."

"Smart..." I was impressed, again.

As we walked inside, lying in the middle of the floor was the biggest dog I had ever seen. His head was the size of my torso.

"His name is Meeko. He's a Bull Mastiff. Just a pup though," she said.

"Just a pup, huh? Hey Meeko," I called very lightly.

As soon as I said his name, he stood up on his four legs and his head came to my chest.

"Goddamn," I whispered, not wanting to startle him. I gave him my hand—palm up—to smell. "We cool, Meeko?" I asked him.

Meeko looked at her, she said something in Japanese, and he resumed his position on the floor. Meeko was not to be fucked with, by any means.

She laughed again and said, "Come on."

We walked through a beautiful kitchen, up into a living room and up another flight of steps into what looked to be another house.

There was a mini-movie screen on the wall, a super king-sized bed, and a Jacuzzi tub in the floor. Between the screen and the bed was a step down with plush theatre seating. People could be sitting watching the screen and you could be on the bed and never see them...CRAZY.

"Make yourself comfortable," she said. "Do you want something to drink?"

"Whatever you're having—" Before I could finish my sentence, she hit some buttons on a remote. The lights went off and the movie screen lit up.

"I'll be back," she said as she kissed me softly on the lips.

I was already busting out of my pants ready to explode. I tried thinking of baseball and crayfish to calm myself down. Then as I looked up, I saw her on the screen...HER OWN FUCKING MOVIE, literally. Not a home movie, but a real porno. My mouth dropped open. Baseball game over. Crayfish dead. Then instead of the normal sound of the movie, from the stereo I heard *Lose Control* by Silk.

Right then my pager starts going crazy. I look down to check it and it's Vince. "Nigga what?!" I said to myself as I cut off my pager.

"Here you go," she whispered.

As I looked up, she's standing in front of me. Her arm stretched toward me with a beautiful baby-blue glass. The glass was sexy. What the fuck is going on? Can a glass be sexy? I am turned on by the glass!

I tried to say thank you, but as I looked at her, I was speechless; words lodged in my through, as she stood before me, steam rising off her body from her intense shower.

A fresh floral fragrance swept through the room. Along with the smell of China Musk Incense and cinnamon, I had no clue where that came from. But it smelled like someone just baked a cake. My senses were on Overload!

Her hair was wet and wavy, her skin glistened as the light from the movie screen bounced off her amazing silhouette. She wore a red towel, barely tucked—and once I noticed it—she released it. Now even though I had seen her body while she was dancing everything was different now, and she was here with me...and me alone. BUT LORD KNOWS I WISH MY BOYS COULD SEE THIS SHIT!

There are no words to describe how sexy this sistah was...from her almond shaped eyes, to her luscious lips, to her plump titties, her exotic nipples, her deliciously deep naval, her hourglass hips, her thick thighs, her shapely calves, her pretty feet. I knew every part because I traced her with my fingertips like a blind man taking it into his psyche.

And, of course, the masterpiece. Dream's beautiful, clean-shaven pussy. As I massaged and tickled those lips, her head dropped back.

I have to be honest. All my amateur experience was out the window. I had no clue where to start. It was all so sensual...so...damn...hot. I was also scared that as soon as she touched me I would cum all over the place...THEN WHAT?!!

"What do you like?" she asked.

I stuttered as she started massaging my "Man" through my pants." I don't know."

She smiled, looked me in my eyes, and said, "Good... stand up."

I was straight under her command. As I stood up, she pulled off my sweater, then my t-shirt. Then she unfastened my belt, unbuttoned my pants. Then she turned my back to the screen and sat on the bed. Dream looked up at me as she pulled my pants down to my boots, pulling my boxers down to meet my pants. As she started untying my boots, all I could think was *damn, I am butt ass naked, rock hard, in a plush crib, with a beautiful woman. Thank you, Jesus!*

And did I say she made a hell of a drink. Just the way I liked it sweet with a little kick.

"What's this drink?" I asked.

"French Connection with Pineapple Juice. It's Hennessey and Grand Marnier," she said.

"It's good...I—"

She pressed her finger against my lips then grabbed my dick and began to lick the head. Her tongue caressed the tip, before she licked and sucked down the side of my dick, playing me like a harmonica. Then she began sucking me like there was no greater pleasure for her in the world. Her mouth was extremely wet, hot, and soft as her lips gripped and slid up and down, side to side, and before I knew it…

"Baby…I'm about to…to…" I moaned.

Then she raised her hand and did something that blew my mind. She gave me thumbs up! Literally stuck her thumb in the air! I came so hard my ears started ringing. My body went into these crazy jerks. I felt like my legs were going to give out. Dream knew exactly what to do. She grabbed and cupped my ass in her hands. This did two things: she was so strong it felt like I was sitting in her hands, and two she now was pulling me deeper into her throat. She slowed down and did a more erotic lick, softer, because she realized that after a brother came his dick was way too sensitive to be grabbing. But the strangest thing happened. My dick stayed hard! Turned on was an understatement.

I felt her giggle, and then she said, "Hey, Mr. Big Dick."

I couldn't speak. She swallowed every drop and seemed to want more.

"Where are you from?" I asked, amazed.

She just laughed, stood up, turned me around, and pushed me on the bed. Then I heard her slide open a drawer then closed it. She ripped a condom package open and slid it on me. Then she mounted me and slowly slid down on my hard dick. Now before this evening, I wasn't a big fan of waterbeds. They moved too much for me. But when Dream began to ride me, I realized that waterbeds are all about rhythm. You have to be in tune with your partner. She put her hands on my chest rode the wave. Every time the wave hit the small of my back, I arched, raised my hips, and tightened my ass cheeks and thrust. Each time this motion occurred, she moaned. And at that moment, that was the greatest sound a man could hear.

"I love this dick, you feel so good," she moaned.

I didn't know what to say. I just liked hearing her enjoying herself, and she felt good, too.

Then before I knew it, we were fucking! Not sex anymore. We were sweating and each thrust took us deeper. I palmed and massaged her back as she rode me like a horse at Pimlico. Then I sat up and started kissing her as we fucked right in each other's face. It got so good I bit her on the neck—almost drew blood and she went nuts! She loved it!

"Do that shit, baby. Hold up," she said as she got up and got on all fours.

Her ass was gorgeous, plump, and round. Once again, I had to bite her…right on her ass. I got behind her, slid in, and started fucking. Her body was so tight, but soft. Her ass rippled up her back each time I hit it. I grabbed her shoulders to drive deeper. She put her head into the bed, put a pillow under her stomach, and put her ass higher in the air. I then stood on the floor.

I was actually making her scream into the bed. I had to remember what I was doing. This was unbelievable! These were college courses, and I was sixteen.

* * *

T.L Rawlings- debuts his first short story which will leave you breathless. Enjoy -the work of a true writing Genius.

www.troy-ghosthost.com

www.myspace.com/troyghosthostrawlings

www.myspace.com/troycalilove

www.myspace.com/ghostinvegas

www.myspace.com/tabootalktour

myspace.com/tabooapparel

A Bowl of Fruit

After I came out of my daze about sticking in nine inches of my eleven and one-half inches into my next victim, Crystal, the white girl who originally invited me to the party appeared.

Recap:

At the office, I witnessed Crystal giving two female coworkers lessons on dick sucking and swallowing with a bowl of fruit. She massaged the banana with the little ball in the back of her throat.

BTS:

My name is Henson Phillip III. I have an alter ego named Devin that persuades all the women to explore our eleven and one-half inch tool. We are a pair of alter egos and personalities that enjoy each other.

The party is in full force. Crystal grabs my hand and leads me to a room, which is actually a walk-in closet. Once we enter this closet, the other two girls from work also enter. Devin, my alter ego jumps in and drops our pants. My dick is standing at attention.

Pause:

Devin is out of control sometimes. But, I love it. I would have never dropped my pants in public. But, Devin will do anything in public.

BTS:

Crystal states, "Henson, I didn't know you were that bold. You usually are low key. If I knew you were ready for this, I would have done you at work."

Devin kicked in again. "If I knew you could handle my equipment earlier and you liked black guys, I would have had you sucking my dick the first day I started this job."

She said, "Henson, that's a bold statement."

"Usually, I get what I want," I responded.

The other two women responded. "Henson, if you can handle all three of us, then you will be the man on the job."

I said, "Handle all three of you? I could handle every girl at this party."

Now, Crystal comes closer. My pants are down around my ankles and she is on her knees. I never wear drawers. So, she has my piece in her mouth, tickling the tiny ball in the back of her throat, just as she did with that damn banana.

Pause:

This is the first time Devin or I have had a blowjob.

BTS:

Damn, it was good. She licks the whole shaft about six times on each side down to my nuts. Then she swirls her tongue around my nuts as if she was licking an ice cream cone. Now, she is back at the head. She inhales it like taking a tote of a joint. She is smoking my dick. Damn, I am loving this. After licking all sides, she starts sucking real fast, turning the dick as she sucks all the way to the shaft. She has my whole dick in her mouth and I am speechless.

Devin kicks in and says, "This is some good black dick ain't it?" Then, Devin pulls the dick out of her mouth.

Pause:

I ask Devin, "What the hell you doing?"

He says, "Trust me Henny. I got this."

I say, "Devin, I got this."

Now we are arguing. We never do that.

BTS:

Devin takes complete control, walks to the other two young ladies, and tells them to get naked. One of them says no. But, the other one does as she is instructed.

Crystal is following saying, "Henson, let me finish. You have not even cum yet."

Devin instructs them both to get on their knees. Crystal and the other young lady complies while the third lady watches.

Devin says, "She must be a virgin, or she scared of this dick."

Crystal and the other young lady continue to comply with Devin. He stands over top of them as they lick and lick. When he is about to cum, Devin positions them both on their backs, heads touching each other, and comes on their mouths, foreheads, in their eyes, and all over their faces. They love it.

As I always say, "I love that Devin."

The End

The Goodie Trunk – Goodie Bag –
That Secret Drawer

My fantasy
My fulfillment
My dick replacement
Is hidden

I masturbate constantly
Alone with my mate
While I am on the phone

Pleasing me
Is
What
I
Do
Best

Everyone else reaching their peak
Is secondary

Madame Butterfly, Lil Magic, Big Blue,
Rock Steady are all loves of mine

Maggie's Madness

I wake up, finger still stuck in my sweetness, Lil Magic still laying beside me, and I'm still shaking.

Recap:

I just broke up with Lil Magic, which is my vibrator, because once I've used it, I get addicted to sex with anyone. I am married with two wonderful little girls. So, I need to behave myself sexually. My name is Maggie.

BTS:

I hear movement in the house. It's my husband. He picked up the children and fed them. He also had some dinner for me.

Pause:

I told y'all I loved this man. He is so good to me even though I am a straight-up hoe.

BTS:

I push Lil Magic under the bed. He hands me my food, then gets into the shower. I eat my food and notice that he has not come out of the shower yet. So, I ask him if everything is okay.

"Everything is fine," he states, but he realizes he has not been taking care of me sexually.

Pause:

Prayer: My mother always said prayer changes things. I have been praying for him to fulfill all my needs and now it's about to come true. Thank you, Jesus!

BTS:

So, he pulls me into the shower. His dick is rock hard and hanging from him like a water hose, just dangling. I step out of the shower for a moment. I get some mouthwash. I step back into the shower, pull him close to me. My mouth is full of mouthwash. I inhaled the head of his dick and started swallowing it.

Pause:

Mouthwash: There is an ingredient in mouthwash that numbs the tongue and, ultimately, numbing the head of the dick.

BTS:

So, as I am giving him the best blowjob of his life, he is panting and moaning, "Mag Mag, Mag Mag." That's his nickname for me. "I love you." I am sucking so hard, he is hollering. I did not realize I only had half of his piece in my mouth until he pushes the other half in. I gag because the numbness of his head had actually made it extremely fat, which is choking me. But, being the expert "Headologist" that I am, I adjust and suck his dick continuously for the next hour. He is loving this and I am so happy to be pleasing him, since I know he will not be cumming any time soon. I need him to put his water hose in my fire because I am burning up in my sweetness. It's begging for attention. Even though sweetness needs attention, I want to please him first. So, I continue to suck his dick and lick his balls. I am turning the dick while I am sucking.

Pause:

Let me explain. As you suck the dick, turn with your hand. But, also with your mouth, go up and down the dick sideways, which will drive him completely crazy. You will get the title "Headologist."

BTS:

As I am doing these moves, he is actually crying. So, I know he is close to cumming. So, I slow down to just licking the head. It's getting fatter and fatter. Then, it happens. He starts yelling, "Oh Shit!" I don't drink this time. I just keep licking slit in his dick, tasting his sweet cum.

Freeze:

He is having a multi-orgasm. All of this is so sweet. I wish I had a camera because he can't handle it. He is shaking, panting, and hollering. Then, he starts saying, "I love you. I love you. I love you. Please don't ever leave me." He balls into the fetal position just shaking.

BTS:

I sit there not knowing what to do next. After he gets himself together, the water hose seems even longer. The head was still real fat. He pulls me to him. Even though I want his dick in me right now, he starts licking my sweetness. Instead of licking the clit first, he inserted his tongue deep into my sweetness and starts doing circles inside of my sweetness.

I say, "Damn, damn baby, slow down."

He slows down. His feet are on the floor and he stumbles over Lil Magic, my clit teaser.

Pause:

I am so embarrassed. What will he say? What will he think of me? "Please Lord, don't let him leave me."

BTS:

He picks it up and looks at it.

I say, "Baby, baby, I can explain."

His eyes get bigger. Then, he turns it on and it makes my favorite sound. I am scared and horny at the same time, which is a weird feeling for me. He gets back into position and continues to lick sweetness. Then, he turns Lil Magic on and puts it on my clit as he continues to lick inside my sweetness.

"Oh my, oh shit! Oh world, oh Lord! OHHHHHHHH!" I am loving this. Now, I am crying. He uses Lil Magic on me better than I use it on myself. "Yes, yes, OHHHHH!" My legs won't stop moving. I feel like I am peeing on myself. But, it's not pee. It's white stuff shooting everywhere. This has to be a dream. I can't catch my breath. "AHHHHH." I can't take this anymore. Then he pulls Tim-Tim out from the dresser drawer.

Pause:

Tim-Tim is my butt vibrator that I used to keep in my car.

BTS:

He shoves Tim-Tim in my ass. I am crying, scared, and cumming at the same time. I am terrified and thrilled at the same time. What will he do next? He takes me off the bed and puts me on the floor on all fours like a dog. He turns Tim-Tim on in my ass then, sticks his dick in my sweetness. I loose it completely and start backing up on his dick like a dog. I back him all the way into the wall. Tim-Tim is tearing my ass up and my husband is demolishing my sweetness. I am still cumming. I start barking like a dog. "Ruff, ruff, ruff!" My husband is smacking my ass as he drills my pussy.

He is saying, "Mag Mag, you have been a bad girl." And, he says he has to punish me by fucking the daylights out of me. Guess what world – I am loving it! I told you my sweetness was my weakness!

Let Me Flow:

I Just Love That Man

From his curly hair
To his sweaty feet
I just love that man
From his tongue
To his long dick
I just love that man
To taking care of the girls and me
To him taking care of my sweetness
I just love that man
Ladies, when you find a good one
Keep him
And Love That Man

BTS:

Back at Howard University, Professor Kindred asked me, "Did I have the results for my experiment?"

I told him, "Yes, but I need to finish up typing them. I will have it to you before the week is out. The experiment results will blow your mind."

The Professor said, "Margaret, I am looking forward to viewing your work."

Now, I am at the library typing, reliving the episodes at the house in DC. Mr. eighteen-inch piece is dancing in my head. The instructor for orgasms, which is me, starts to play tricks with me. I am not sure what my husband did with Lil Magic and Tim-Tim after our encounter, but, I still wear Madame Butterfly and I have this new gadget called Big Blue aka Bullet. It's a bigger version of the Bullet. It touches the "Lil Girl in the Boat" and it's also long enough to go inside my sweetness. I love this toy. It puts a new meaning to "motion in the ocean."

As I leave school, I decide to go back up to Rock Creek Park. This is where the experiment all started. I pull up to the exact spot I parked when I started this venture. I pull out Big Blue. I need to revisit what happened at the house in my mind. So, I recline my seat again. I put Big Blue all the way in my sweetness. Then, I climb in the back seat. I turned Big Blue off first. I lay in the back seat. I adjust Big Blue just right to tear up the pussy and it does just that. It fucks me like my husband did that night. Wow, this is fantastic. I have both my feet hanging out the back window. I am just enjoying myself too much!

Let Me Flow:
Visions of My Sweetness

I please myself anywhere
 Toys
  Are
   My
    Friends

I also Love a Big Dick
 My sweetness
    Begs
     For
       Attention

Visions of Sweetness
 Is what
  I am

BTS:

While Big Blue is tearing up my sweetness, I hear noises close to my car. I hurry to adjust myself and sit up. I pull my legs back into the car and pick my head up to see what's going on. After I get myself together, I realize it's just some old man and his dog. I am not sure what he saw. But, he has the biggest "Charlie Brown" smile on his face. So, either I assume he saw my toes at attention or Big Blue stuck all up in me. My sweetness is my weakness.

I finally get up and get back in my front seat. I adjust my seat and turn the car on. I tap my sweetness and Big Blue with the baby wipes and put Big Blue in my glove compartment. I put my pretty purple panties back on and pull off. I go to the college to finish my paper there. While I am typing, this young girl keeps looking over my shoulder. Then, she asks, "Excuse me ma'am, is all that true?" I replied, "Every word." She replies, "No way!"

So, we go into a deeper conversation. I tell her, "People call me Maggie." She told me, "My name is Quida." She said, "If all you wrote about is real, how did you experience it without getting fucked or eaten?" I said, "Hold up. Meet me later today and I will take you to the house in N.E., D.C." As I was talking to her, a tall good-looking dude starts to wave me over. I didn't know his face. So, I said, "You must be talking to her." He said, "No, I'm talking to you." So, I go closer. I still can't figure out who he is.

Let Me Flow:
Strangers

Last night I loved a stranger
It was the beginning
Of my wet dream
Was it right
To make love to a stranger
There was nobody
To take care of
Sweetness

BTS:
Now, I go over to the guy. I still can't figure out who he is. Then he states, "You are already married. So, I can't marry you."

Pause:

This is Mr. 18 inches with clothes on. Why is he at the college?

BTS:

I said, "Oh, now I remember you." He said, "I really enjoyed you work. You are the best I ever had." I said, "Look, I need you to keep that between us. And, I also need a favor." He said, "Anything for you Maggie." I told him I need him to meet Quida and me at the same address so I can finish my experiment. He said, "Tell me the date and time."

Pause:

I will have Quida to experience what really turns a man on because I need to stay married and stop whoring.

BTS:

So, we agree to meet at 6pm tonight in Northeast, D.C. I ask Quida if she is ready to see if I was lying or not. She gets nervous and stuff. I said, "Sweetie, are you a virgin, on your period, or just scared?" She said, "I am 1 and three." My response, "You a virgin and you're scared?"

She said, "Yes Maggie." Now, I'm puzzled because I had only planned on watching this time. I didn't plan on participating.

Let Me Flow:
Decisions

Choices and Decisions
Go hand in hand
Choices are what I make
Decisions are what I have to live with

My choices have not been good
My decision to make better choices is what
I try to live by

BTS:
Quida agrees to go. But, she doesn't agree to participate. We both leave the college. I take her address because I have to pick her up. So, as she gives it to me, I tell her to wear some pretty panties. She responds, "Why?" "Because men love pretty panties. So, wear a pair."

When I pull up to Quida's apartment building, it's 7:30. She lives on the first floor in a complex called Park 16. It's on the Maryland side of Southern Avenue. I get out of my car and enter through the foyer of the building. She is actually sitting in the foyer. She looks totally different from when I met her with her schoolboy glasses and plaid skirt. She has on a mini skirt and the smallest tank top I have ever seen. She wears about a size six or eight. But, this top has to be about a size two. Her titties are about to burst out of her bra and run out of the shirt. So, we greet each other, "Hey girl. What's up?" I said, "Come on. We have to get to the location so I can finish the experiment." Professor Kindred gave me three extra days to turn in everything. So, we walked to the car and she said, "Nice car Maggie." My response, "It's just that. It was a gift from my husband for fucking his brains out one night."

Pause:

Ladies and Fellas: Good fucking will get you material things such as cars, boats, clothes, and money before the person ever realizes what they are doing.

Deeper Explanation: When you have mastered how to fuck so intensely that the opposite sex can't do anything but smile when they see you, you are fucking well.

BTS:

So Quida said, "So Maggie, you are telling me that good fucking can solve all my problems needing a new car, money to live off, and paying for my apartment?" "Yes Quida. All of your needs could be met if you fuck the right one. He will provide all your needs. Just think, most women give it to their man free and get an "I love you baby" in return. After I fucked my husband so good one night, I asked for a Mercedes. The next day, that's what I had."

Now we are in front of the house. I have this look on my face and Quida asks, "Maggie, are you ok?" I said, "Yes Quida. But I am afraid once we go in here, I will loose myself. Quida, I have to tell you something." She said, "What is it Maggie?" I said, "Please Quida, keep this between us." She said, "I promise Maggie." "Well here it is Quida. Are you ready?" She said, "Just say it Maggie!" "Ok Quida, I have an addiction." "Ok, well, just go to rehab." "No Quida, not drugs, or alcohol. Quida, Quida, I'm addicted to dick!" Her mouth drops. "How are you addicted to dick? Is there a cure?" I said, "It's not that I am really addicted to dick. I am addicted to orgasms. Orgasms drive me crazy. I have to have at least 2-5 per day just for me to feel normal." Quida responded, "Now Maggie, that's a problem."

Pause:

Let me explain how this happened...

History: It started when I was 18. I was washing myself and ran a hot washcloth over my clit, realizing the pleasure that arose from touching it. I touched it again and again and again. Then, I was shaking and I had these uncontrollable leg movements that drove me crazy. But, I also loved it. Crazy and in love at the same time— wow, what a wonderful way to feel. So, after that, I got addicted to touching, feeling and rubbing my sweetness. As I always say, "My sweetness is my weakness!"

BTS:

Quida stands there in total amazement. Her last question is, "Maggie, do you love yourself?"

Pause:

My sensitive side: I started crying, sobbing uncontrollably when she asked me that question. I never knew what love really was. I was always taught if a person takes care of you, its love. So, that's what I did for the children and my husband did for me. So, I considered that love. My grandmother and mother always said that love came with material things. So, do I really know what love is? The answer is NO.

BTS:

Quida said, "Maggie, we can learn a lot from each other. You teach me about sex and I will tell you what I know about love." We hugged and I said, "It's a deal."

So, we go into the house. It's the same as when I was here last time. The same lady that greeted me before said, "Hey Maggie. You're back and you have a friend." I said, "Yes, her name is Quida." She said, "Since you're not a rookie to this, you show her where everything and everyone is." I said, "Ok, we will see you later." She responded, "I am sure you will see me later. Today, I am the orgasm teacher. In about forty-five minutes, my session will begin in the basement. Hope to see y'all there." I said, "Maybe if we are not caught up in something." She responded, "I know that's right!" Quida and I were on our way.

Let Me Flow:

Corruption
Why do I have this girl with me?
I am a freak by myself
Do I think having her here will stop me?
Or am I tripping and cumming
All at the same time

Let Me Flow:

Why not
I am already here
I am already horny
I don't have panties on
I don't have morals
My sweetness begs for something that size
My mouth, the gripper

Needs something to grip
If you can think of a
Reason not to
Please tell me
If you can't
Then WHY NOT

BTS:

Once we started walking around, I could hear some familiar voices. I tell Quida, "Let's follow those voices." Quida just nodded. The voices were from Albert and Lil Dank. As we are walking through the house, we are getting closer. I can hear Lil Dank saying these words like, "Come here girl. Show me what you working with." He actually sounded like he was James Brown. So, we froze in the corner. We still had a good view of the action. Lil Dank was really packin'. His penis was huge for a lil man. He was barely five feet tall. His dick was bigger than his legs. Quida coughed and said, "Damn!" I put my hand over her mouth. Then the expression on my face said, "Yes Maggie, one last time." We watched Lil Dank in action. The young lady that he was talking to was about five-foot-nine and really cute. Once Lil Dank got her to agree to what he said, he convinced her to bend over. She must have been blind!

Side note:

With the size of his dick, I was surprised that her first move would be doggie-style.

BTS:

Quida and I love this. Evidently, she is a voyeur also.

Meaning: Voyeur – love to watch other people have sex. I am also an exhibitionist. I love to be watched while having sex.

BTS:

So, as Lil Dank was drilling her from behind, his dick is so long, he doesn't even have to stand up. He has he backwards and he is sitting on the bed. She loves this. Actually, I love watching this. Quida has this look of fear on her face and I whisper in her ear, "What's wrong?" She says, "She thinks she has to pee." I say, "Please Quida, can you hold it for about five minutes?" She said, "I don't know."

Pause:

Learn your body ladies. If you learn how to control your muscle so that you can hold your pee, it also works when you are having sex. You can tighten and loosen your muscle in your pussy and ass, which will make you have some wonderful sex and orgasms. That will also make your mate beg for more when you control those muscles in bed.

BTS:

So, Quida and I just watched in total awe as Lil Dank tears her pussy up. She is calling him names like "Big Daddy" and "King Kong." She's right about King Kong because his dick is not only long. It's huge in width. As he continues to thrust, I slip my finger into my sweetness. Then, I touch the little girl in the boat. She moans. I moan and Quida is in the corner whimpering. As he continues, we continue to make sounds. I thought he had heard us. But, he keeps on thrusting. She starts yelling, "Yes, yes, yes!" Quida's face is flush red. I think she peed on herself. She starts shaking and shaking. Now, everyone is yelling. I am also yelling because the lil girl in the boat has me shaking. I put my hand over Quida's mouth. I go in my purse and get some baby wipes so she can freshen up. We get out of sight so Lil Dank can't see or hear us. Quida revealed that she didn't pee on herself. She said, "She thinks she had an orgasm." As I look at all the white fluid on her legs, I told her "that's exactly right."

Pause:

Most women have not had an orgasm even though they have had sex numerous times. Some women are forty years of age and have never masturbated or used toys. So, when a woman has cum for the first time, most times, she doesn't even know it!

BTS:

Quida said, "Oh girl that felt so good. So this is what you are addicted to, this constant shaking, and this warm white liquid running out of you?" I said, "Yes Quida." She said, "Now, I understand." So after we both freshen up with the baby wipes, I asked Quida was she ready not only to get taught how to turn a man out, but was she ready to get turned. She replied, "Yes!" As she said that at the top of her lungs, Lil Dank comes out of the room towards us. His dick was still out and hard as a brick. I don't know how someone that short could have a dick that's almost longer than his leg. Totally Amazing! When he gets closer, he says, "Hey Maggie. I missed you the last time you were here. But, I heard you enjoyed yourself. They nicknamed you "The Big O Instructor" for your performance.

Recap:

When I was last here, I was looking for the orgasm class! I could not find it. So, I sat down and watched the men get off. While I was watching, I attacked the lil girl in the boat and she responded with orgasm after orgasm. Everyone was watching when I opened my eyes. So, they thought I was the orgasm instructor and started clapping for me.

BTS:

So, Quida's eyes are stuck on his dick. I try to act as if I don't even notice it. But, as he gets closer to me, he stands in place and lets out a sigh of relief. I ask if everything is ok. He says, "Yes, but, I need a favor, a big favor." I said, "What is it Dank?" He responded, "I am kinda embarrassed to ask Maggie." I said, "Come on Dank, you helped me to get the research done that I needed for Professor Kindred." He whispered in my ear. He said his dick was swollen because he had not cum in a month. He asked if I could help relieve the tension. Then he said, "If you say no, I'll understand. I know we are just friends and you are married."

Let Me Flow:

Just Friends

With a piece like that
Almost touching the floor
How could we be just friends?

The way you handled that girl
While you knew
We were watching
How could we be just friends?

By giving me access to
This house and letting
Me enjoy myself
How could we be just friends?

The way you know
My sweetness begs for
Something that size
How could we be just friends?

BTS:

I tell Dank I need a favor from him also. "I will relieve all your tension. But, you have to agree to let Quida watch and participate and promise not to hurt her mouth or her insides because she is a virgin." Dank said, "Of course she can watch, Maggie. I will not hurt her insides because I plan to be inside you."

Let Me Flow:

Inside of Me

This big dick has plans for me
The things and moves I can do
With this – Inside of Me
The inside of me is
Where it should be
I know I might regret it

But for now

I want it

Inside of Me

BTS:

Lil Dank said, "Maggie and Quida, lets go to the third floor. You two go up to the third floor and go through the red door on the right hand side. I will be there in a few minutes."

Quida and I went upstairs and waited. Quida said, "Maggie, I am nervous, but excited." Then she said, "Maggie, I really want to feel Lil Dank inside me. I enjoyed what he did to that tall girl. She loved every minute of it. Maggie, if I am going to loose my virginity, I want to loose it in a big way. I want Lil Dank all up in me. When I leave this house tonight, I want to be crawling out to your car."

Pause:

Freak Potential: I can assure you that Quida's grandmother, mother, and father are ho's. Freak runs in the family. It's in the genetic makeup.

BTS:

So I really show Quida how to enjoy herself. I show her how to masturbate so her coochie can withstand penetration.

Instructions: Here is how to get a quick nut: Insert two fingers in your mouth and lube them up real good. Put those two fingers on the lil girl in the boat aka your clit. Gently rub up and down. Lube your fingers again. Go from left to right. Do this for about three minutes. Then, since she is ready, attack the lil girl. Go faster and faster and faster. That way, the sensation will build. Then the moisture from the lil girl will start to shoot out. Then you know you have gotten an "A" on your assignment.

BTS:

Quida does just what I instructed. She is so caught up that she never noticed Lil Dank was in the room. We both watched her as her eyes reached the back of her neck. Her eyes are rolling so much, they look like she is about to go straight crazy. Then she starts yelling and screaming. Dank and I are already playing with each other. He has is hands in my sweetness. I have my hand and tongue on his third leg. Damn, it's just that big! I need to loosen up my own coochie because a piece this big is going to kill me. But, I have to do this before Quida. If he takes all his frustrations out on her, she will be hurt for life –not able to have children and maybe even a hysterectomy.

Let Me Flow:

It's D Day

Its time for the dick

I know I am ready

But I didn't know the

Dick would be

This BIG

BTS:

Once Quida finishes screaming and shaking, she opens one eye and gets a glimpse of Lil Dank's hand in my sweetness. Then she opens the other eye and can see my hand and tongue on the third leg. She is rather bold now. She comes over and helps me suck on his third leg. As I am licking the sides, she is licking the head. His piece is too big to deep-throat. So, we both tag team on the head. I have half in my mouth. She has some in hers.

Our lips never touch each other. Lil Dank loves this and so are we. I slip my hand back into my panties and tickle the lil girl in the boat. Then I get so aroused, I take my skirt and panties off. Dank is looking at my sweetness and notices that it is clean-shaven, which makes it so tempting. Lil Dank said, "I have never seen a bald pussy. Come closer and let me taste it, touch it, and tease it."

Pause:

You would have thought he had seen a ghost the way he looked at my pussy.

BTS:

He examined it, licked it, smelled it, put his nose inside of it, caressed it and just played with it. As I always said, "Keep your sweetness ready for action at all times!"

Side note:

Black women and Black men don't shave as much as other ethnic groups. For some reason, we think that's taboo. On another note, that's why the only time some of us get "treated" to oral sex is on our birthday, holiday, or when our mate is drunk.

BTS:

But my sweetness and I stay clean-shaven. I am sometimes getting eaten three times a day.

Oral Service Announcement (OSA) – If you constantly want your mate to keep the tongue and lips on your private areas, even if it's not a special occasion, keep it shaved – not any designs on it, just bare. I use some gel called "Coochie." It's the best. It makes my sweetness as smooth as a baby's ass. I use "Dude" on my husband. His skin is so smooth down there; I suck his dick about twenty times a week. So, take this OSA and keep the hair off those areas.

BTS:

So, as Lil Dank is having the time of his life with my sweetness, he tells me to sit on his face. I do as I am instructed and I tell Quida to sit on his dick. This will be the easiest way for her to experience penetration without him pounding in her. She agreed. So I get up first. Then I put Quida on top of him. We are holding hands to keep our balance. I lower Quida down on his massive piece. She is crying. Tears are running down her face. I ask, "Is she ok." She said, "I am enjoying this so much. But, it hurts too.

Pause:

I am kind of mad because I wanted that big dick in me first. I have not problems with being second. But, now I am third. I hope he has enough energy for me.

BTS:

Now I am focused again. So, as I ease Quida down on Lil Dank's piece, she is screaming, hollering, cussing, and fussing. So we grab hands as Dank is working both of us. He is eating my pussy as if it is the last supper and he about to die. He is probably the best eater of pussy ever! Quida is still crying. So, I explain to her how to jump up on the dick. She jumps up once, jumps up twice. She is truly enjoying it. I can't tell if Dank is because I can't see his face. My ass is on his eyes. So Quida jumps up again and it goes in the wrong hole. She is frozen.

Pause:

Caution: If you have never had anal sex, work your way up to it with butt plugs and vibrators, gels and lotions and anal pleasers. Don't ever just think that you can take it in your ass without preparing your mind for penetration, your muscles for flexibility and your mouth because you're going to be yelling.

BTS:

Lil Dank throws me on the floor and Quida is yelling. I am also crying now because he threw me. As I get up, my job is to get this big dick out of Quida's ass without having to call 911. I actually see tears streaming down Dank's face because his dick is hurting. So, I grab my purse and pull out my KY Jelly. It is not working. But, I have a special product for real tight situations. It's called Anal Ease. I keep this in all my goodie bags cause sometimes you get caught in tight spots. So, as I put Anal Ease on Quida's ass, I am actually getting turned on for two reasons. One, as I am rubbing his dick with both hands, he loves it. Two, I have never been this close to another woman's body parts.

Pause:

I am actually laughing inside. She knows he should be in my sweetness instead of her tight virgin ass.

BTS:

So, Anal Ease does this numbing thing, which makes it easier to pull the two of them apart. Since his piece is so massive and she is a virgin, it is really taking some time to release them. Now, Dank is yelling, "Are you almost finished Maggie?" I said, "Wait a minute Dank. I'm trying." Quida is no longer crying. She is actually smiling and wiggling. The Anal Ease must have numbed her ass. She is moving more and more. Then, out of nowhere, she starts saying stuff like "Yes I am loving this big dick." You should have seen the look on Dank's face. He was still hurting. So, as he kept moving around, he finally pulled himself out of her. Then, he had a big sigh "Ahhhhhh!" Now, the floor is filled with his juices. It has to be almost forty ounces on the floor like somebody spilled a bumper of beer. Quida asked Dank if he was ok. He just nodded. Then he said, "Never again will I make the mistake to go in a virgin ass without being well-oiled up." I defended Quida, "Dank, she didn't mean to hurt you." He said, "I know." So I told Quida, "Lets make it up to him." She said, "How Maggie?" I told her, "Just follow my lead." I grabbed Dank's hand and led him to the bathroom. Quida followed. They had a shower that five people could fit in.

It had a handicap seat where we sat Dank on. The head on the shower was portable with a long handle and five settings. The setting I chose was "vibrate." I lathered his whole body and Quida lathered the massive piece. We washed him up real good. He enjoyed every minute of it. I positioned myself and told Quida to follow me on the shower floor on my knees. I took the vibrating head of the shower and put it on his third leg. I tell Quida to start licking. Quida does as instructed. I massage it with both hands. I have Quida to keep licking and licking. Then, Quida states, "Maggie lets change positions." I tell her, "Sure." We changed positions. But, I am not in the mood for licking. I have played with my pussy so much today; I need that massive piece in me right now. So, I position myself so this massive piece could enter me. Dank is smiling now as I ease my sweetness on him. The more I ease the bigger the smile gets. My smile is actually getting bigger too. Finally, I can get what I have been wanting for a while.

Reflection:

I could not have Broomstick in me. Mr. Eighteen only wanted a blowjob, but Lil Dank is actually entering my sweetness.

BTS:

So, as Dank slowly puts it in, I start to realize this piece is actually bigger than I thought. There is no small part. It starts fat and stays fat. But, I love every bit. "My, my, my…this is good." It's hitting the most sensitive parts of my sweetness and my inner thighs because he only has the head in. My lips and inner thighs are contracting and it's giving me chills all up to my braids. Now, he shoves more in and I am bracing myself. He puts more in. I scream. Quida comes over and grabs my hand as he serves me his massive piece. He grabs my legs and pulls me back. I am begging now. "Please let me go!" Quida is cheering him on. "Get her Dank! Get her!" I really don't like to lose control. But, I think I am about to. He grabs me. Quida grabs my hands and he buries his whole face in my sweetness. I am screaming, hollering, shouting, saying, "Damn, Damn, Damn!" all at the same time. It's happening. It's so powerful it has to be a double multi. I am trying to hold on. "No, no, no…yeah, yeah, yesssss! Damn!" I love every minute. But, it's also tearing me up. But, I love it.

Flashback:

Visions of this big dick have been on my mind since I was eighteen years old. I saw our neighbor, Mr. Steve through the window of my friends' house. I was peaking in the window to see if she was ready to go to the go-go. Her mother and our other friend's father, Mr. Steve, was in there with her tearing her ass up. I was frozen because he saw me. He smiled and kept on doing her. She was hollering and shouting at the same time saying stuff like, "Big Daddy "and "Big Pappa." Then she yelled out, "Big Dick Steve." I snickered and she heard me. She said, "Who's out there?" Big Dick Steve said, "Ain't nobody out there." Then, he winked at me. He pulled his dick out of her. I said, "Damn!" I got so weak in the knees that I fainted. When I came to, Mr. Steve and my two friends were standing over me. So, from that day on, I have always dreamed about a Big Dick like Lil Dank's.

BTS:

So, as I said, I always wanted what I am getting right now. Every minute is like the first time. The size of his piece makes my sweetness seem like it a virgin. It's tearing me apart.

Let Me Flow:

Tears flowing

Juices Leaking

Smiles and tears at the same time

Happiness and hurting

He was killing me softly with his piece

Killing me softly

With his piece

Making me forget about everything with his piece

BTS:

Quida comes over to me. "Maggie, you ok? It seems like its hurting you to keep moving backwards on that piece of his." I tell her, "Girl I have been waiting for this piece all my life and I plan to enjoy every bit of it." Then I move back further. Dank thrusts even harder. I can feel him up in the middle of my chest. He is up here where my lungs are. I am about to choke from him pounding into my sweetness.

Pause:

I learned this trick years ago. Ladies listen up! In order to handle a real big dick like this, you have to stimulate your clit while he is in you. This moistens your sweetness so you can take in more dick.

BTS:

So, as he is pounding my sweetness, my lil girl in the boat is on fire. She starts to let my juices flow, which in turn lets him put more dick in me.

I love every minute. I start talking trash. "Faster! Harder! Claim this sweetness! This is the best you have ever had! You can't handle this pussy!" He reacts and starts shoving harder saying, "Yeah Maggie, you have never had a real man until now! This is the biggest and best dick you will ever have!" I respond, "Prove it! How long can you last? Since you have the big dick, do you know how to use it?" This makes him mad and I can tell because he is punishing my sweetness. I am loving every inch. He is moving so fast, as if he is the "Six Million Dollar Man." He is running through sweetness like he is a track star.

Let Me Flow:

Damn

My sweetness is on fire

It's getting all the attention

It deserves

It's cumming

It's farting

I am singing I am sighing

No flashbacks just flash forwards

And all I can say is

DAMN!

BTS:

Quida is staring at me with the look of a deer caught in headlights. She can't believe I am taking all this dick.

Pause:

It's really too much. I just don't want her to get any more until I am completely satisfied. Call me selfish. You can even call me a freak. But Maggie and Sweetness get what we want.

BTS:

Now Dank looks like he is getting tired. I tell him "Don't punk out on me now. I am not finished." I realize he is not tired. But, he is about to get off. His eyes start to float. His movements are going slower and slower. He is closer and closer. Then it happens. He starts to talk more and then this hot wave of juice explodes in me. It felt like an ocean mixed with a steamy hot shower, just totally incredible. It's so good I start to dream – what if? What if?

Let Me Flow:

What if I can't leave?

What if I don't want to leave?

What if my husband finds out?

What if he burns me?

What if Quida tells on me?

What if I am never satisfied?

What if I start to go to church?

What if I stay a ho for life?

What if I get myself together?

What if I stop cheating?

BTS:

After I come out of my daze, Quida has this look on her face. I ask her "Is everything alright?" She said, "Yes, but, I am concerned about you." I said, "What about me?" She said, "You're married Maggie. You should not be doing these things."

Reflection:

My grandmother was a freak. My mother is a freak. I am the only married woman in my family. I don't think I know what having a monogamous relationship means. My grandmother cheated on my grand dad. My mother cheated on my dad. And, now I am cheating on the best man I have ever known. Cheating and being a freak run in my blood.

BTS:

I respond to Quida. "Let's talk about this later so I can tell you why I act like I do." Quida agrees and says, "Ok Maggie."

Now Dank is just lying on the floor. I nestle up to him. He said, "Maggie you ok?" I said, "Yeah." He said, "For real, I never thought about you being married. I just wanted you from the day we met." I said, "For real Dank?" He said, "Yeah. I thought you were fine and then once you spoke, I could tell you were not like the other girls Howard. There is something special about you that I don't think you even see Maggie." Now I am getting all teary-eyed and I nestle a little closer to Dank. Quida gets on the other side of him. He starts to pour his heart out to us. He said that all his life he had to prove himself to everyone because he was short. I was the only one who accepted him for him.

Pause:

He just don't know that I could see how big his dick was when I met him cause he kind of wobbled as he walked because his dick was just as big as his leg.

BTS:

So he goes into telling us about him feeling that he has to prove something to everybody because of his small size. I am lying beside him and he starts kissing on me. Now that Quida is all bold, she starts kissing on him. He goes further and further down, and ends up at my sweetness. Then he starts this move that's new, even to me. He inhales my clit. It disappears into his mouth. "My, my, my!" Quida is now licking down his back and smiling up at me. Now she is licking and licking as if she is trying to lick his skin off. But, it's turning him on because his tongue starts this circular motion inside my sweetness. But, he does it differently. He swirls his tongue left and right. Then, he starts doing circles. I am about to lose it. I push him away.

Let Me Flow:
I shouldn't have
I did it
I rode it
I sucked
Damn I enjoyed
But I shouldn't have
I should not have been here
I should have not sucked it
Enjoyed it or
Rode it
I should have
Thought about this
Thought about my kids
Thought about my husband
Thought about the life
He provides for me
I shouldn't have

BTS:

So as Dank is taking me to dream world, my whole life flashes by me.

Reflection:

I start thinking about growing up poor and my mother trying to make ends meet by sleeping with men for money. Then as a teenager, I did the same thing and my mother told me that grandma did the same thing. But, they did it because they were broke. I am just doing it because I enjoy it. Lord, something is wrong with me.

Let Me Flow:

Rhythm of Cum

It flows through my body

Each time I have an "O"

I am searching for a multi "O"

Some would call me a ho

Some would call me a freak

Some would even call me nasty

I love the rhythm

That an "O" does to my body

It makes my toes curl

My hips quiver

My spine arch

Let me tell you

I call myself "O.C."

That means Orgasm Chaser

'Cause I chase "O's"

All day

Every day

BTS:

As guilty as I feel, I still feel like I own this big dick. So I block out all sense of reality and loose myself in lust. I tell myself this is right and then I start yelling for Dank to fill me up with all of him because I need it now. I start talking trash. "Stop eating me and let me ride that dick. What? You can't handle it Dank?" He stops eating and Quida lets my arms go. Then I lay him on the floor. Instead of getting straight on top, I get on top sideways.

Pause:

Let me do a demonstration:

Lay him down on the floor. Turn your body sideways. Then sit. This will give you total control and it will explore a part of your sweetness that is rarely touched. Usually the only time this is touched is when you use certain toys.

BTS:

So as I am on sideways, he is enjoying himself totally, because Quida has my bullet next to his prostate, which is driving him CRAZY.

Pause:

Ladies, put your bullet by his prostate. He will love it. The first time you do it, give him a blowjob then put it right there. He will have the most powerful multi-o. He will be crying, singing your name, willing to pay your car and house note without asking.

BTS:

Now Dank is going absolutely crazy. It's even more powerful than I thought. He is moving his legs. His speech is slurred. He is breathing hard and looks like he is going to faint. I tell Quida to hold up. He yells, "Don't stop! I am about to…" Cum sprays all around the room. He is holding his piece like it is a water hose and he is putting out a massive fire. His cum goes everywhere—on the ceiling, on the floor, and it's running down the wall. "Got Damn!" He screams. Quida and I just look because we have never seen that much cum in our entire lives. We all lay on the floor totally satisfied, totally exhausted.

I am about to take a nap. Then I realize I have to get home and do my paper since it is due tomorrow to Professor Kindred. I tell Quida we have to go. Dank comes over and hugs me, then thanks me. He said, "Maggie, thanks for the Nut." I said, "Why are you thanking me?" He said, "Because when I am with a woman, she is usually the only one satisfied. But you Maggie, made sure that I reaped the benefits too. And for that, I want to thank you. Also, Quida, I know you want to join a certain sorority. I will take care of that for you with no initiation. I will just make a call. And Maggie, anything you need while you're here at H.U., just let me know. From tickets to football games, fashion shows, or concerts, you will be free in the front row and have backstage passes. Thanks for treating me so special. I am forever in debt to you ladies. I owe you big time." Now Quida and I look at each other and hug. I tell her we are friends for life. She agrees. I tell Dank I will see him tomorrow in class. He hugs me again and whispers in my ear, "I will never tell what happened here." I get out of there. Quida is riding shotgun. I speed to her house. We rode in total silence. When we arrived, Quida said, "Thanks Maggie for everything. You are a true friend. I will see you tomorrow. Now, get home to your husband and children."

I start on my way home. I am doing a little bit over the speed limit. Then I notice police lights behind me. I am thinking, "I can not get a ticket over there in Southeast D.C. How can I explain to my husband why I am even here?" So, I pull over and the officer comes up to the car. "Miss, I need your driver's license and registration. I got my license out of my purse and my registration out of the glove compartment. Once I gave him all the information, he asked me to step out of the vehicle. I am real nervous now. I don't know what's going on. Once I am out of the car, he escorts me to his car. I said, "Officer, what's wrong? What did I do?" I am totally in panic zone. He said in a smooth, calm tone, "Ms., you are not in trouble. I need to ask you a few questions. So, please get in the front seat of my cruiser." I had already turned off my car and locked it. I got in the front seat of the cruiser and he pulled off. I am scared and horny at the same time.

Pause:

I am scared because I don't know what's going to happen next. I am horny because I can't get Dank out of my mind.

BTS:

Now we are about two miles from my car. He pulls over and parks. He turns the lights on in the car. Then he states, "Margaret, I have been needing to thank you for a while." I am dumbfounded now because I don't know what he is talking about. He states, "We met about a year ago." I said, "Sir, I don't know remember you." He then pulls his dick out. It's nice. But, it's light and dark, which is weird. But, its rock hard. He says, "Now Margaret, you don't remember this dick?" I am actually getting scared for real. He must be some pervert talking about do you remember my dick. Then he said, "Margaret, I pulled you over for speeding and you had a vibrator in your ass." I said, "Damn. Officer Jones?" He said, "Now I am Lieutenant Jones."

Recap:

It was about a year and a half ago. I was pulled over for speeding and I had my vibrator, Tim-Tim, in my ass.

I told the officer to follow me to a side road a mile up the street. I sucked him so well, skin came off his piece, and he paid me $100.

BTS:

I said, "Hey Lt. Jones. How have you been?" He said, "I am good. Have you been good, Margaret?" I said, "I've been trying." He said, "Let me tell you this. That was the best blowjob I have ever had in my entire life. The reason my dick is two colors is because after you sucked the skin off of it, it had to heal and never turned back to the original color." I said, "I am sorry. I did not mean to hurt you." He said, "That's fine. But, here we are again. I am going to give you my card in case you get pulled over by any other officers and they will let you go."

Pause:

It's a get out of jail free card! I love being Maggie!

BTS:

"But, I need something from you." I said, "What is it Lt.?" He said, "For old time's sake, can you do what you did again?" I said, "Sure." I bent my head down and showed him some of my new skills. I sucked and licked. Then as I inhaled his piece, my tongue got as far back to his asshole and licked that, too. He reclined his seat back, pulled his pants down to his boots, and let me have my way. I did the circular motions and one of the new skills I acquired, letting the lil ball in the back of my throat tickle the head of his penis. He was loving every bit of it. Then I put a Fisherman's cough drop in my mouth and just started slobbing it down like a slurpee-up and down, down, and around licking and spitting and licking and licking. Then he finally reached his peak. I just put my tongue out and let him cum on it. Then I put my tongue back in and let it ooze down my throat. He pulled his seat back up and had tears in his eyes. I said, "Jonesy, what's wrong?" He said, "I think, I think, I think I love you. I said, "Now, Lt. We can't have that. You know I am married." Lt. Jones said, "That's why I'm crying. If you were not married, I would be asking you to be my wife right now. Margaret, I have dreamed about you since I met you a year and a half ago. I have actually been looking for you. Then, I see you today. I don't know if its fate or just luck. But, I am sure glad it happened." I know I need to get out of this car and get home. So, I tell the Lt. now that I have his card, I will call him sometimes, maybe give him some of my sweetness. He got all excited. His dick shot back up to attention. He then said, "Yeah, I would like that." I said, "Lt., can I go now?" He said, "Yes Margaret." Then I licked my lips, gave him a peck on the cheek, and exited the cruiser. I get back in my car and proceed to go home.

Let Me Flow:
The things I do
Are not right
The choices I make are actually foolish
The situations and places are always dangerous
My mind process
And my thought process
Are off balance
My need for sexual pleasure
Is getting the best of me

BTS:
I am now back in my car and I have this feeling of guilt again. Why do I keep on putting myself in these

situations that could end my marriage and ultimately, my life? If my husband finds out I have been cheating on him, I know he is going to kill me. I need to come to my senses because this is getting out of hand.

I fix my face up and my clothes and finally make it home. As I am driving, I am praying that my husband is not home. I really can't face him right now. As I pull up, I don't see the company truck anywhere. I am relieved. I get out and dash into the house. The girls are in the living room. Rojena runs up to greet me. "Hey momma. How are you? How was school?" Then Renee comes and just hugs me. "I am glad you are home Mommie." Then she states, "Now the whole family is here at one time." I didn't realize what she said until I got upstairs and my husband was already lying in the bed butterball naked, dick hard, and looked like it was fat as a fire hydrant. He stood up and grabbed me. "I am so glad you are home. I have been wanting your sweetness all day. The girls have been fed. Now, I need something sweet to eat. Come her Mag-Mag." I am scared and horny at the same time. Let's call it Scorny—scared and horny.

Reflection:

I just left Lil Dank, I mean Big Dick Dank. How can I let him eat me smelling like someone else?

BTS:

Ladies, this is when you have to be quick on your toes. I went to the dresser and got some Extreme Pleasure in his favorite flavor, peppermint twist. It is an orgasm enhancing crème from my girl Stephanie, the toy lady. They make you feel like you are going to lose your mind. Once I put it on, he starts licking and licking as if he was licking a dreamsicle from the ice cream truck. I am sweating. He is smiling. It's getting more intense and he started licking down my legs. He turns me over and makes love to my ass with his tongue. He states, "Mag-Mag, I want some ass tonight." I say, "Hold up a minute." I go into my goodie trunk and get some Anal Ease.

Pause:

Anal Ease is a product that is used to loosen up the ass so penetration will not hurt. By putting Anal Ease on my ass and Extreme Pleasure on my sweetness, this will be some of the most fulfilling sex for both of us.

BTS:

So, I put the Anal Ease on and he slides right in. It feels so good. Now he starts counting, "One, two, three..." It's a half hour later. He is on two hundred and still tearing my ass up. I am enjoying every minute of it. My husband can sure tear my ass to pieces. An hour has passed and he is still screwing me. He has not cum yet. So I start doing Kegel with my ass cause I got skills.

Pause:

Kegels is the method of contracting your muscles. Most women use it in their coochie. But, I have learned to use it in my ass also.

BTS:

Once I start the Kegels, he is hollering, "Yes Mag-Mag! Yes Mag-Mag! Work that ass! Goddamn! This is some good ass." Then he lets off an "Argghh" sound and I feel his cum seeping out of my ass. But, he is still hard. He starts counting again. This time his thrusts were more powerful. He flips me over to put my legs behind my head and gets on me backwards.

Let Me Demonstrate:

Picture this – Roll over into a ball. Have your mate stand over you and insert his dick inside you, which gives him all the pleasure of completely turning you out. He is turning my ass and me out.

Pause: Women – when an ass is fucked right, your orgasm is just as powerful as a multi. Sometimes, it is a triple multi from the intense penetration and the Tabooness of having a big piece of meat in your ass.

That's why what Maggie do is Taboo.

BTS:

So as he continues to fulfill all my needs, I start to flash back and have a reflection.

The man loves me, takes care of me and the children, and fucks me like there is no tomorrow.

Let Me Flow:

Intense – Pounding

Uncontrollable urges

Every sense and body part on fire at the same time

Tears and smiles
Pleasure with a hint of pain
Enjoying it and smiling
Hollering and cheering
Talking dirty and saying "I Love You"
Hair falling out your head
And standing up on your back
My sweetness is definitely my weakness

The End

Feenin in 1990

Total fulfillment

Is what I offer

Your thongs around your neck

Is what you will become

Addicted and unconscious

Is how I would describe our sessions

Exotic and erotic

Is how you describe me

A stallion and a gentleman

Is how you describe me

To your friends

Wet and crazy

Is how I describe you

That's why what I do is taboo

90 Degrees

It was only mid-October and it was hotter than July on this particular night. My central air in my condo did not work. If I had known it was broken, I would have gotten it fixed. But, I had just flown back into town and the young lady I had met before I left also lived in my building. She greeted me as I walked into the building and asked, "If I wanted some company."

Pause:

She was a brick house – caramel complexion, nice breast, real firm ass, and a pair of lips that only thing you could think of is "I want those lips on my dick."

BTS:

I told her I needed a shower and asked if she wanted to join me. She said, "No. I will just watch some TV until you get out."

After I got out of the shower, she got in. So, I got in the bed and fell asleep. I didn't realize the air was out until around 12:45am. I was sweating. I also realized that Tendi, my neighbor, was lying beside me. I needed some relief. So, I started to taste her sweaty juices from her pussy.

Sidenote:

Sweaty pussy is the best tasting pussy. Fellas, eat your woman after she comes from the gym, jogging, or aerobics. That is some of the best stuff. Also, if she takes water aerobics or swims, it's something about chlorine and pussy that makes the taste amazing.

BTS:

So, after tasting this good pussy, it was time to have my way with her other lips. I moved up to have her deep throat me.

Pause:

Let me completely satisfy her before I get mine.

BTS:

So, I went back to the sweaty pussy and ate and licked and licked and swallowed and licked all the way down to her ankles and back up. I licked her cute little titties and kissed her passionately like Victor kisses Ashley on The Young and The Restless. As I kissed her again, she started trembling. Wow, she was having an orgasm without me even touching below her naval.

Class:

All women should take this class. She controlled her orgasm in her mind not her body. Damn! Men need this class, too.

BTS:

So, as I watched this in amazement, she told me how to increase my own awareness of a woman's body. I listened. I wanted her to deep throat my dick. But, instead, she told me to come up to the top of the bed. Mind you, she was still lying on her back. She told me to stick my dick in her mouth under her tongue. Then, she wrapped her bottom lip around it. The top lip automatically closed down on it. Then, she massaged the tip of the head with her tongue and drove me crazy. This was fantastic! Then, her oversized tongue started massaging my balls. She had not even started and I was about to cum. Damn, I couldn't hold back. I started thinking about snow, college, car crashes and I still couldn't stop it. It was gushing out all over and she loved it. She started talking to my dick, as I was cumming, saying, "This is the best pair of lips you have ever had. Say it. Say it." And I said, "Yesss!" I was having a multi-orgasm in her mouth and she was still swallowing and talking, talking and swallowing. She got the dick right back up. I can't even remember her name. But, I think...I think...I think I love her.

Let Me Flow:

Dick in her mouth
Swallowing and talking
At the same time
Crying and enjoying myself
At the same time
Wanting to marry her
But curious
Where she learned these skills
I don't care
Girl, I Love You

BTS:

I fell asleep in the fetal position because I'm drained physically from the tremendous head job and emotionally because of the New York trip and seeing Tessa act as if she didn't know me. It all just took a toll on me.

It's Monday morning. Tendi is still here. I need her out of my space. Not only do I have some business to take care of, I need to be alone for a while.

Pause:

Being alone is not a bad thing. There is a difference in being alone and being lonely. Learn the difference.

BTS:

So, I had to get her out of here without hurting her feelings or our friendship. Earlier in my life, I would have just thrown her out. But, now that I am older, I try to respect and care for women in a different way. I looked at myself and said, "Who is this impostor? Mr. Roarke only cares about himself."

So, I let Tendi know that I would love to see her later this week maybe for dinner and dancing. She started to get all perky. "Roarke, I would really like to do that with you."

Then I tell her, "Thanks for not taking advantage of me in my sick state of mind over the weekend."

"Roarke, I really like you and I am glad to be here when you need me. That's what friends are for, right?"

Pause:

Fellas, you have to learn how to get into a woman's head. Once you get into their mind, their thoughts are your thoughts. They speak and don't even realize that you put those words in their mouth.

BTS:

So, after stroking her ego by getting in her mind, she said, "Roarke, I need to get home." She gathers her clothes and her purse and goes into the bathroom. After about fifteen minutes, she comes out dressed and ready to go. She came over and hugged me. She gave me her business card, which also had her home and pager numbers written on the back. She told me she would see me Friday if I were available. We hugged and she walked out of the door.

I realized that I got into her head so well that she thought leaving was her idea. I am a bad man!

Now that she's gone, I can focus. I need to contact Dré. I have not spoken to him since we left New York City. I also have not heard from the ladies. So, I get my phone and answering machine from the closet.

Pause:

Never have your phone or answering machine in sight or in reach of your company. You never want anyone other than yourself answering your phone or checking your messages. Also, if you can, turn the volume off on both of them to avoid any conflict. That is in the Handbook on page 6.

BTS:

As I turn the volume on, it stated that I had sixty messages. Damn, I did not know the machine could hold that many messages. So, I started listening.

"Hey Roarke. This is Shaleeha. Is everything alright?" Twenty messages were from her. After going through hers, the next one was from Toni.

"Roarke, call me. I want to make sure you made it home safely." She left about twenty messages. Then I hear Shake's voice.

"Hey Roarke. This is Shake. You need to call me ASAP. I have some news for you." Then I hear Dré's message.

"Hey Roarke. This is Dré. I just wanted to check on you. I saw the look on your face when you saw Tessa. Roarke, don't worry about her. You can have any woman in the world. Remember you are Mr. Roarke. You are what fantasies are made of."

I start to smile. Dré is my ace-boon-coon. He always had my back.

So, I pepped up and called Shake first. "Hey Shake. What's up?"

"Are you in town?"

"Yeah."

"We have a family emergency. Meet me at M's house in about an hour."

"Okay."

I returned calls to Toni and ShaLeeha to let them know I was fine and that I would call them back later. Then I called Dré and told him to meet me at M's house in an hour.

Pause: Confused – I showered. But, I am confused. What emergency occurred while I was away?

BTS:

So, I got dressed and left my building. I was really stressed. Thoughts, emotions, and fear took over me. What if it's my mother? What if one of my sisters is hurt? I had been so selfish with my own needs that I forgot about everyone else.

I pulled up to M's house. All of my brothers and sisters were already there. There are six children – two boys and four girls. I am the youngest and sometimes, I think, the worst of all of my mother's children. So now, I have a guilty complex because I don't visit my mother as much as I should because of my new business.

Pause: Stop lying! It's because I'm a ho and my mother keeps telling me it's going to catch up with me and I believe her. I just hope it's not while I'm living. Black folks think we are going to live forever. That's why we live the way we live and never have insurance.

BTS:

When I got to M's house, I knew something was wrong. Everybody has that look on their faces. I said, "What's wrong?"

Shake said, "Something major, Roarke."

Let Me Flow:

My Mother
Queen of the Nile
Mother of the world
Banker, Father, Good Friend
The essence of Jesus
Is only greater
Helpful and Saintly
Intelligent and Thrifty
She is my Everything

BTS:

I came out of my fog and Shake grabs my hand. He said, "Come up to M's bedroom. She wants to see you."

I enter the room and M said, "Sit down Courtney Edwards." Wow, she said my full name. I know I am in trouble now. She never says my full name. I sit and then my four sisters and brother come into the room. My mother continued. "Courtney Edwards, I hear you have a baby by Ms. Alice's daughter from up the street. I don't believe it. Tell me that I am right."

Recap: Before I can answer M, I have to recap. I usually don't do girls in the neighborhood unless I met them somewhere else. Never sleep where you eat.

BTS:

I said, "Naw M, I don't have any children by that girl. She slept with some of the fellas. But, not me."

"I am not through with you." Then she invited all my siblings to chime in. All my sisters asked me to leave their girlfriends alone and asked if Dré could do the same. My oldest sister claimed she did not have any girlfriends because I slept with all of them. Then, my middle sister will not even speak to me. She claimed that all her girlfriends have slept with me.

Shake just nodded his head while saying, "Roarke, you a bad man."

Recap: I learned my playa ways from Shake after my father left when I was fourteen. Shake became my role model or father figure. Shake was a ho at sixteen and I followed his example. Remember, he was only three years older than I was. Shake actually set up my first piece of pussy. That was why I fell in love with tall girls. She was six feet three. I did not have anything to say to her since I was only fourteen and she was twenty. So, Shake said, "Give her this drink." I gave her Jack Daniels mixed with NyQuil cough syrup. I put it on ice. She loved it and let me have my way with her. Afterwards she sucked me dry and rode my young dick for hours. I was hooked and in love at the same time. That's the first time I was really feenin.

BTS:

So after everybody finished telling me off about my sexual escapades, I shook Shake's hand, hugged my sisters, kissed M, and said, "I'm trying to change. I will not do y'all friends any longer." I left the house and drove to my "thinking place" which is St. Elizabeth's Mental Hospital or St. E's. I pulled up and I saw couples and some of the patients walking around. I get out and sit on the grass overlooking the Washington Monument. I got deep into thought and started to pray.

Dear God,

It's me Roarke. I know I only come when I need help. So, here I am. I have some issues that I need to resolve by myself. But I know I need you.

After I got my thoughts together, I sat back in the car. I turned on the radio and heard Phyllis Hyman singing "You just don't know what I been going through. You just don't know. You just don't know." I paused, reflecting, and start singing with Phyllis. "They just don't know."

Let Me Flow:
Lost Turned Out and Just Plain Crazy
I don't know
Who I am
Why I am here
I am not just searching for a lost love
I am searching for my soul
My actions are crazy
My disposition is lost

I am searching like a drifter
These thoughts have made me
Lost, turned out, and just plain crazy

BTS:

So, when I came up for air, I got out of the car and sat back on the grass, gazing at the sky. Tears stream down my face. I didn't' even know why I was crying.

Flashback: I go back in time. That hot summer night in July, Tessa and I at St. E's on the hill watching the stars, me playing with her clit. She was caressing me so tightly. Man, can I bring back that moment?

BTS:

I am stunned because I heard someone talking to me. The voice said, "Sir, sir, are you alright?" I come to and look up; realizing the person calling me sir is about my age. She was a beautiful young lady. I asked her why she called me sir.

"I don't know your name."

"My name is Courtney."

"I'm Iris."

I shook her hand and said, "Nice to meet you."

Then, she took over the conversation. "You look like I looked a couple of weeks ago."

"How is that?"

"Like not only did someone break your heart, they stepped on it and put it in the trashcan." I looked at her with a stunned face. "I am correct. Right?"

"Yes you are correct. Can we leave here and go sit down and maybe have dinner?"

"I will follow you to your house and we can drive my car."

Pause: This took me aback – she followed me to drop off my car – not the other way around?

BTS:
She said, "Yes. How far do you live from here?" I said, "Not far. I live in the Towers by Sam's Carwash." She replied, "Iverson Towers?" I said, "Yes." She said, "I live across the street in Carriage Hill.

Pause: That's a little too close for comfort for me. But, I will play along because I think she is really sweet and I need a friend right now.

BTS:

So, she followed me home. I parked my car and got into her car, which was a Volkswagen Jetta. I strapped on my seatbelt and adjusted my seat.

"Courtney, just relax. I am not out to hurt you. Where would you like to eat?"

"Chesapeake Seafood."

"Cool. I was thinking that, too."

Recap: The only women that get to eat at Chesapeake usually pay me or have to sleep with me.

BTS:

But, Iris seemed different. She deserved to be treated like a lady. There was something different about this one. I couldn't put my finger on it. But, it was something different about her. Oh, let me describe her. She was about five feet five inches tall, caramel complexion, nice tight package, gorgeous eyes that made you melt, and her voice and demeanor were just so soothing.

I started the conversation off with, "Iris, what did you do to pick yourself up after the bad breakup and miserable feelings?"

"Cort? Sorry, may I call you Cort?"

"Sure."

"I went out and did a whole lot of dudes and got him out of my system."

"How did that get him out of your system?"

"Because he was the best sex partner I ever had. When I went out and had some terrific fucking with a few other guys, I realized that's all it was. It was good sex. I can get that from anyone. But love; now love is a different Beast."

"I understand."

We finally arrived in front of the restaurant and she parked her car. I got out and opened her door. She thanked me and then said, "You don't usually do this. Do you?"

"No, I don't. But, how do you know?"

"Cort, I date your type. It's all about you. Right, Cort?"

Pause: She was trying to reverse the game. She shortened my name. Now she was talking to me as if she has known me for a lifetime. Who could she be? This was the role I usually played in life.

BTS:

So, as we started to talk about sex again, she started to tell me about her turning men out and having them babbling like little children and crying like babies. I told her she had skills to reverse the tables on a man like myself.

"Cort, what makes you so different?"

"What makes me different is I only think with the head above my shoulders

"That does not make you different. That makes you smart, but, not different." Then she says, "Cort, the things that I could do with you and for you will drive you crazy. You might even start paying because you will be so fulfilled."

Now, I am back on my game. I responded, "You must be trippin to think that you can turn me out and have me babbling and crying. Girl, you really don't know who you talking to."

"Cort, you really don't know who you're talking to. I eat men like you for breakfast."

"Iris, I eat lil girls like you as a mid-day snack." We both start laughing. "Thanks Iris. It's fun talking to you."

"The feeling is mutual, Cort."

We continue to talk. Then the food comes out. I ask her to hold my hand while I say a prayer.

Pause: Yes, you are reading correctly. I always pray before I eat. Sometimes I just talk to God as if He is sitting beside me.

BTS:
She holds my hand. But she started the prayer.

Dear Heavenly Father,
I want to thank you for sending Cort my way.
Bless his heart and his pathway.
In Jesus' name I pray
Amen

I am sitting at the table with tears running down my face. I tried to wipe them before she saw me. She saw my tears, wiped my eyes, and asked, "What's wrong, Cort?" I tell her it's nice to find someone that prayed for me. She said, "Cort, that's what a real woman does. She prays for her man."

Pause: Wow! Who is this girl, Iris? No one has ever really prayed for me except my mother. Momma could have made that gospel song *Somebody Prayed for Me* 'cause each time I would see my mother, she would tell me, "I'm praying for you." This is how the song went:

Somebody prayed for me
Had me on their mind
Took the time to pray for me
Then the chorus is:
I'm so glad they prayed for me

BTS:
So, she stated, "Cort, you have not been with a real woman until she adds something besides sex to you."

"Iris, I agree. I think it goes both ways. You have to bring something to the table."

After we finished eating, I order two Blue Hawaiians, two Sex on the Beaches, and two Strawberry Daiquiris. We sat and talked and drank from each other's drinks. We were laughing and enjoying ourselves. When I came back up from laughing, I felt lips around my piece. But, they're sucking on my jeans. I was past tipsy. So I did not realize that Iris was under the table. She pulled my dick out and was grinding on my nuts. I was loving it. So, I stopped her and she came up for air. I asked her if she would like to go back to my place.

She said, "No, we can go over to my place."

Let Me Flow:

I don't know

What's going to happen?

I don't care what happens

I want to enjoy

This night

I want to enjoy

This woman

And I think

I think

I like her

BTS:

I asked for the check. When it came, she grabbed it and said, "Cort, this one is on me."

"Iris, I will go back to your house only if you start calling me by my nickname, Mr. Roarke."

"Mr. Roarke, like on Fantasy Island?"

"Yes."

"They should call me Ms. Roarke because I make fantasies come true. You will see that when you arrive at my place. Mr. Roarke, the only thing I ask is that you let all of you inhibitions go 'cause I plan to take you to places you have never imagined."

We rushed out of there and to the car. She French kissed me and we headed to tongue city. We were kissing so hard, you would have thought we were teenagers. I was on sex overload 'cause my dick was as hard as fifty five boxes of jawbreakers. I was no good. I felt like I had blue balls. So I slowed down and told her, "Lets hurry up to your place." She was flying down the highway. We got to her place in about three minutes flat. It should have been a fifteen-minute drive.

She told me to run behind her. So I followed suit. She was running like she was a track star. I got to her once we got to the third floor. I was actually tired. But, my adrenaline was off the charts. My chest was pumping so fast, not from running up the stairs, but from the anticipation of what's going to happen once I got there. My mind was playing tricks on me and I was loving it.

Pause: Real foreplay – for men it's the chase. Women, learn how to make him chase you for your goodies. When a man chases you through the motions of exploring you, it really means he wants you and not just sex. The truth test to that is to make him jerk off before y'all have sex. This will determine if he is after you as a person or after you just for sex. If he is after you for just sex, after he jerks off, he will just leave. But if he is into you, he will stay. Try this one ladies.

BTS:

I finally reached the destination and see that she has an apartment filled with mysteries. Let me define mysteries. She had sexual items lying around and she had given them all names. Each time I picked one up, she would call its name and say what it did. I picked up one item that looked like a rabbit and she said, "That's called Bugs Bunny" because when she used it, she was hopping around. Then I touched another item and she said, "Don't get too close to Mister."

"Mister what?"

"I call that piece Mr. Feel Good 'cause when my real Mister can't do the job, I can call on the artificial one." It looked like something painful with numerous pricks. It scared me and turned me on at the same time.

Pause: Me scared? Who was this fella? Mr. Roarke ain't scared of nobody or anything.

BTS:

So, as she introduced me to these objects, I ended up in her second bedroom. So, I asked her if she had a roommate.

"No."

"Well who does this bedroom belong to?"

She laughed aloud. Then she reverted to calling me Cort and said, "Cort, do I scare you? This room is for special guests like yourself."

"Why do you consider me a special guest?"

"It's a swing over there by the closet. I would like you to be the first one to test it out. Also, Cort, you will have to earn the title "Mr. Roarke." I cannot call you that until you've earned it."

"I doubt that you will ever earn the title "Ms. Roarke" unless you have some super natural skills."

"Once I get on that swing, you will think that I am Wonder Woman and you're one of the bad guys 'cause I plan to turn you out."

I don't know if I should get comfortable or run. This young lady is a different breed of woman. Toys, whips, a swing, and she was not intimidated by me.

Let Me Flow
I think I am scared
Someone that makes me wonder
Someone that keeps me on my toes
I think I am scared
From whips and chains to
Creams and lotions
Down to that swing
I think I am scared

Her sneaky ways
To her thinking
She controls me
I think I am scared
To her devilish smile
And her soothing voice
Damn – I know I am scared

BTS:

So, she positioned me to get on the swing. She actually lifted me up onto the swing.

Pause: Damn, she was mighty strong. I had to make sure this was a woman. Most women are not that strong.

BTS:

So, I started looking at her neck to see if there was an Adams apple and at her feet to see the size. She had no Adams apple and small feet. So, I pulled her to me and just grabbed her in the pussy.

"What you doing? Since I am strong, you think I am not a woman?"

Freeze: How did she know what I was thinking?

BTS:

So she stripped naked. I could not breathe. Her body was so fine.

She said, "Cort, say something."

"Damn!"

"I work out. I lift weights. I ran track in high school and my older brother is a professional boxer. So, my body is a combination of them all – strong thick legs from track, muscular arms from lifting weights, and strength because I can box."

Now I was really no good because if I didn't treat her right, she might just kick my ass. So I rethink my strategy. Where was the Players Handbook when I need it? So as she started to come closer, she started to take off my clothes. As she took off my shoes, I pulled my shirt off. She pulled my pants off so hard I fell out of the swing. She picked me up.

I started to kiss her and she pushed my mouth away and stated, "I don't kiss Cort. Let's get started." She pushed the swing and I said, "Woo." She pulled the string up close to her mouth and started to deep throat me. She was sucking and swirling. Then she pushed the swing back. Mind you, my dick was feenin for attention. As the swing came back up, she held it again and started to lick ferociously. I was in total shock. I was also feeling intense pleasure. She had skills that were equal to a porn star. Damn, this girl was on fire!

Let Me Flow

She has toys
And skills
Looks and brains
An apartment
And money
I don't know
But, just maybe
Just maybe
She is
My equal

BTS:

As I was feeling a sense of urgency and a sense of loosing control, I came back to my senses. Mr. Roarke has returned—bigger, better, blacker, bolder, and just plain nasty. So, when she pushed the swing, I grabbed her, put her in the swing, put the straps on her legs and then I paused. I started calling her "Nasty Girl." Then, I asked Nasty Girl, "Where are the condoms?"

"The small ones are in drawer one, medium in drawer two, large in drawer three and extra large is in my purse."

"Why are the extra large ones in your purse?"

"Because very few guys are that big. So, I only have two."

I got her purse and now my dick was so fat, I could not get the head in the condom.

She yelled, "Wow! It's really fat."

I pulled her to me and just stuffed it in her mouth. She gagged and I shoved harder. She adjusted her mouth and tongue, and went to work on it. She was swirling, swishing, and just sucking.

Pause: Back in the day, I would have gone in bareback. But, I have had enough diseases and infections. I had everything from syphilis to yeast infection and urinary tract infections. Yes, fellas, we do get those, too. So cover your dick!

BTS:

So, she licked, sucked and talked to the dick and said stuff like "Let me taste you. Cum, big daddy." I was enjoying it. Then I had a flashback.

Flashback: Late night, Barry Farms, South East, DC—me getting my dick sucked by this red girl and she burnt the shit out of me with her tongue.

Yes, you are reading correctly. She gave me a STD with her mouth!

BTS:

So, I pulled out of her mouth, rolled the condom on my dick, and got to work. Her legs were tied—one behind her head, the other behind her back. So, I got pussy for days. I entered and started handling my business. But, it was something extra special about that pussy. It was extra hot as if steam was coming from it. I didn't want to hurt it. I just want to please it.

Let Me Flow
I just want to please her
I am being gentle
I am taking my time
My rhythm is emotional
My stride is slow
I am cuddling her

And talking

As I am stroking

I just want to please her

BTS:

She looked into my eyes. She looked so deep; I think she could see my soul. Her eyes were piercing my skin. It was like the sun while you are lying on the beach. Even though I am dark chocolate, I felt like I was getting a tan. She was piercing my heart with her eyes. This extreme pressure was taking me out of my game. So I stopped looking at her. We embraced and switched positions. She got in the swing and told me to tie her legs up in the air so they would be above her head.

Picture this – It was a total clear angle of all her goodies including her ass. I forgot to tell you about her breasts. They were perfectly round with a wide nipple about the size of a quarter. I was having visions of quarters coming out of a slot machine in Atlantic City. So, since I was a gambler, I put the left quarter in my mouth. Then I stuffed the right quarter in my mouth. As I was trying to get change from these quarters, she moaned really hard and said, "Cort – I mean Mr. Roarke, that's my spot."

I continue to lick and suck on the quarters since she confirmed that was the spot. We got more and more into the act of turning each other out. This session of foreplay was incredible even to me. It had been almost two hours and I had not yet entered her. I wanted to flashback. But, the present will not let me. Damn this was some powerful stuff she was putting on me. Only Mr. Roarke could handle stuff this powerful. As we proceeded into all the different paradises she had in store for me, I wanted to flashback. So, I paused.

Let Me Flow

Tonight I loved a stranger

I just met her

I am at her house

She has sucked my dick

I am about to enter

Tonight I loved a stranger

She has had numerous mates

And so have I

My mind should be on something else

But it's not

Tonight I loved a stranger

From the swing

To the condoms

To her knowing a lil bit too much

About sex

Tonight I loved a stranger

BTS:

So, as I came back to Mr. Roarke, I let her know where we were going. I stuffed myself into her tight, waiting pussy and I gasped. It seemed like for life because it was hard getting in. But, once I got in, I realized her muscles were not in the typical place. They were in further up. She was gripping my dick with her pussy muscles around the end of my dick backed up where my balls were. It was an incredible feeling. So incredible, I thought I was about to—I pulled out. I was about to cum. I had only been in ten minutes. Reputation—I cannot cum for at least an hour. My reputation would be shot. Actually, I would be average. Mr. Roarke can never be a BM— a basic man. Never!

"Hey Roarke, what's wrong?" she asked. "Did it get too hot in there for you?"

"Never. You are talking to Mr. Roarke. It's never too hot." So I got myself together and realized that I had to do something I had not done in a while. I had to think about what's in the "Playas Handbook" for total freaks. I think it was on page 109: *If you have tried all the tricks in your bag – Try these...*

1. Dump Truck – put it in her ass.

2. Dick Aerobics – make your dick so hard, you can't cum.

3. Go Postal – Do some stuff that you don't even understand—break down—Go CRAZY!

So, I took the advice of number three. I went postal, straight crazy. I had her up in that swing and I went to the Dump Truck. To my surprise as I inserted my dick in her ass—I just shoved it all up in her and she started to stop the swing—she moved up and down my dick backwards. Let me remind you I was packing eleven inches. She acted as if it was only five. She slid up and down it as if she was climbing a tree backwards. It was not tight like the typical ass, but, her muscles were as strong, or stronger, than most pussies that I have been in. As I backed away, she clamped down on my dick really tight with her ass muscles and I completely lost it. I attacked it like never before, pounding—putting in work—hitting that ass, again and again.

Then she gripped it extra hard and looked me in my eyes and yelled, "Roarke...Mr. Roarke, cum in me right here, right now."

All I could do was to do as she said like she had a spell on me or something. There I was, cumming on demand. I was flooding her ass with my seeds and she was jumping up more and more. Her muscles got tighter and tighter, refusing to let go. She had turned the tables. She was now fucking the fucker!

Pause: I have to get out of here. I have lost all control. I have lost my own warped sense of reality.

BTS:

I lifted her up. I had to find my pants and I was running down the hallway. It's time to get out of here. I finally got to my condo. I ran all the way home! You would have thought the police was after me. Once I got to my place, I actually got down on my knees and started praying.

"Dear God, Stop me from doing foolish stuff. Keep my dick in my pants. In Jesus' name I pray. Amen. Amen. Amen."

I went to the bathroom. I needed a bath. So, I get everything ready to take a bath.

Pause: I always take long baths. I feel somehow they will change what's going on in my life. It's like that old commercial for Calgon bath bubbles. The catch phrase was "Calgon, take me away," and the person would disappear in the bath bubbles.

BTS:

But, I could not disappear–not even into the bubbles. I was still here. So, I said aloud, "Calgon, take me away!" The only thing I could hear was Rene and Angela on the radio singing *Your Smile*. Then, I heard Rick James singing, "A teardrop fell from my eye yesterday." Then, The Average White Band was singing, *A Love of My Own*." I was choked up.

Let Me Flow

Crying again

Why me

Why not me

I have hurt people

It's time for me

Crying again

No emotions – and no class

Miserable, lonely, and heartbroken

Disgusted and scandalous

Crying again

BTS:

I finally got out of the tub because I heard the phone ringing. I picked it up and the voice said, "Roarke, Roarke, are you alright?"

"Who is this?"

The voice said, "Boy, this is Dré. What's wrong? I got to your mother's house and you were already gone. You have not returned calls from your pager. Your car was not parked in the usual place. What's up?" Before I could respond, Dré said, "I'm on my way." He hung up. I got dressed and within ten minutes, Dré was walking through the door.

Pause: Dré had keys to my place. So, he did not need to knock. He just put his key in and came in.

BTS:

Then he said, "Roarke, put your gear on. We are getting out of here."

"Where we going?"

"To this new club called The Spy Club in DC. It's hot! It has the jazz group named Spur of the Moment. They are bad! Nothing like some good jazz to get your mind off things."

I put my clothes on and we were on our way. We stopped past this spot and played lottery numbers. Dré always kept a number in and he hit plenty of times. So, as we went in, we saw Kelvin Trainer, an old friend of mine from Barry Farms. Everybody called him "K.T." He had a high Philly like Big Daddy Kane, and draped in gold like Mr. T. But, he was my boy. He asked if he could roll with us. Dré was hesitant, but, I said, "Come on."

So we were on our way to The Spy Club. As we rolled towards the bridge, we were drinking beers, and laughing and listening to music on the radio. Then, we heard popping sounds and Dré pulled over and said, "Who the

fuck busted my damn car window? Is everybody okay?"
Then, he said, "I'm gonna have to fuck somebody up!"

Next thing I know, I couldn't feel my arm.

Dré said, "Roarke, you okay?"

"No Dré. That was not a brick that busted your window. Somebody just shot at us."

Just then, a small car pulled off real fast.

Dré said, "I am going to go get him."

I hollered, "No Dré! I need to go to the hospital. I've been hit."

Dré looked over at me as I was getting weak fast.

"Hold on, Roarke." He put the car on two wheels as he sped towards the hospital.

Pause: When you are in the hood, the police do not come unless you're dead. Since I wasn't dead yet, Dré was taking me to the emergency room.

BTS:

We arrived at Greater Southeast Hospital and I was about to faint. I ran into the emergency room shouting, "I am shot!" I didn't know where I had been hit and I was terrified. Nurses and doctors ran to my rescue, rushing me to a gurney. Then the police came in. They stripped me naked trying to find out where the bullet was, as I fade in and out of consciousness.

Dré parked the car and finally reached the emergency room. He's yelling, "Where is my boy Roarke? You okay?"

I said, "Dré, stay here."

The doctor yelled, "If you are not his immediate family, you have to leave!"

I said, "He is. He is my brother." Then I slip into unconsciousness.

I heard Dré saying, "Roarke, Roarke! Y'all better save my boy or I'm gonna tear this place up!"

K.T. was holding Dré back saying, "Let me call Roarke's mother."

Dré punched him in the face and said, "She needs to hear this from family and she don't know your ass!"

My mother arrived at the hospital with my oldest sister. The look on Mom's face spoke volumes.

Immediately, I said, "M, I was not doing anything wrong."

"Then how'd you get shot?"

"I don't know," was all I could say.

Pause: I am actually scared of my mother. My whole life, I have always tried to make her proud of me and this definitely was not a proud moment.

BTS:

So as she hugged me and kissed me on my forehead, my sister broke down crying too. Now all of us were crying.

Dré walked in and my mother grabbed him and said, "Dré, you are supposed to take care of my son."

Dré said, "M, I don't know what happened."

The doctors and nurses came in and surrounded me. They put all of the visitors out of the room in order to prepare me for surgery.

Dré said, "Roarke, you are going to be all right. You know you my boy for life."

My mother kissed me and said, "I love you, son."

Then my oldest sister said her special saying. "Soldier to soldier, I love you."

Everyone left the room and I was nervous because I never had surgery. I had only been to the hospital one time in life. When I was in kindergarten, I got hit by a car. I was with my sister on Martin Luther King, Jr.

Avenue when the car hit me, and I was rushed to the hospital. So, this hospital thing was truly scaring me.

A young nurse came in along with a candy striper. They both were cute and they said, "Courtney, it's going to be fine. Surgery will get the bullet out of you and you will heal in no time."

Pause: Since they were cute, normally, I would have hollered at them. But, that was not on my mind.

BTS:

I just smiled. They had to shave my pubic area so that the doctors could shoot dye in my body so they could see where the bullet was. As the nurse pulled back my covers, she had the clippers out and realized she did not need to shave me. She looked surprised.

Pause: I have no pubic hair. I shaved it all off after catching crabs years ago. Now that I know how much it turns women on, I plan to keep it that way. I get my dick sucked because of it. Women love something different and a bald pubic area with eleven inches of dick – that's different!

BTS:

That kinda took my mind off of the surgery for a minute because she called the candy striper back into the room and they just admired it until the doctor came in and asked, "Is he ready yet?"

They both stated, "Real ready."

They wheeled me into the operating room. The dye that they put in me was making me hot inside. Not just hot – I was burning up inside. They put me under the X-ray machine that was supposed to tell the doctor where the bullet actually was and what type of bullet it was. I am vomiting from the dye and the X-ray machine seemed like it had been turned up to a thousand degrees.

Let Me Flow

Dr. Jesus

It's me

Courtney Fitzgerald Edward

I need you now

I need you right now

Please heal me

In Jesus name

I pray

Amen, Amen, Amen

BTS:

I had to get my prayers in. The doctor called out to another doctor. "Something is wrong," he said. "Something is wrong!" I was having an out-of-body experience. They couldn't be talking about me. What could be wrong? About ten doctors and some nurses rushed in to the operating room. I was vomiting. But, I was unconscious. They are trying to figure out what's wrong. Tears were running down my face. It's as of I was floating, looking down on myself. I couldn't be dead yet. I knew I could not have been an angel because I had been a devil on earth. God does not allow them in Heaven.

Pause: I have a flashback. I think about when Dré and I had just got on the train coming from New York City to Union Station when the young lady that sat with me said, "Heaven does want you." I am hoping this is true because I am blanking out completely. I whispered, "I love you, Mom."

BTS:

IVs was hooked up to me and folks were standing around me. I was hoping this was not heaven because I was not ready to go. There are so many things in my life that I have to straighten out.

Someone said, "Courtney, Courtney...Mr. Edwards, how are you feeling?"

I finally came out of the fog and realized I was in the hospital. I woke up completely and immediately begin to vomit, again and again. I was butt-naked with only a sheet covering me as the nurse and the candy striper washed me up. The doctor explained what was going on.

"Courtney, we could not get the bullet out of your arm safely without hitting a nerve which would have made you have no movement in your fingers or arm or both. So we had to leave it."

I asked, "So, when are you going to try again?"

"We're not. You will have to live the rest of your life with the bullet. But, you should be alright. The IVs will prevent infection such as gain green, etc." Then he went on to say that I had to stay in the hospital for a few days and that he would be back to check on me later. He shook my hand and said, "Young man, the angels were on your shoulders."

"Why do you say that, doctor?"

"If the bullet had been an inch over, it would have hit your heart and we would not be having this conversation."

I shook his hand and thanked him before he left.

"Young fella, you have been given a second chance. Please make something of yourself."

"I will, sir."

Pause: I was actually mad. He didn't know me. He didn't know I had already made something of myself.

BTS:

The doctor left, leaving only the nurse and me in the room. I asked her if I could get up and go to the bathroom instead of peeing in the bedside container.

"I will have to help you."

She pulled me up. I started to walk slowly since I am hooked to the IVs. I got to the bathroom and as I am beginning to pee, I noticed she was holding my dick.

I said, "Excuse me, do you do this for all your patients?"

"Just hold on to the wall."

I peed for about three minutes. I am glad she held it because I was weak from standing up that long. I grabbed toilet tissue so I could drain it. I washed my hands and eased back into bed. The candy striper had changed the sheets and pillowcases. She was now sitting in the chair by the window. I am feeling very vulnerable right now.

Let Me Flow
What is this feeling?
Nervous – timid – scared
Unsure of myself
Once I was not only a mack
I was Mack Daddy
Now I am here
With two women
And I can't even talk
I don't know if it's
The medication
Or is it just me
I hope it's the medicine

BTS:

I laid in the bed; the pillows are propped up. I asked the ladies what their names were. Before the candy striper could say her name, I thanked the nurse for her special services.

She said, "You needed my help. My name is Akinnesha."

I laughed a bit. But, I am still sore from the surgery.

Pause: There was an era for black folks when all the children that were born in that five-year span had names that ended in "nesha" or "esha" like Keisha, Neisha, Laqueisha, etc.

BTS:
She said, "What's funny?"

I said, "I had a thought that was personal."

"I hope you were not laughing at my name cause my mother put my grandmother and aunt's name together to come up with it."

I am really laughing now because my mother's name was a combination of my grandfather and grandmother's name. I tell her that and we are all laughing. The candy striper tells me her name is Kerra.

I state, "That's different."

"So am I."

We sit and have idle conversation and I asked, "Can I use the phone?"

They both said, "So you can call your girlfriend?"

"No, before I got shot, I actually had a date. I stood the young lady up since we met and she still calls. So I feel that I can at least tell her the truth this time." So, I remember the number. Kerra dials the number and I get the phone and said, "Nicole, this is Roarke."

She blurted out, "What's your excuse for not picking me up and breaking our date for the tenth time?"

"I was shot."

"Damn Roarke! Can't you think of something better than that?"

"For real, I am in Greater Southeast Hospital right now. Speak to the nurse."

I put Akinnesha on the phone and she confirmed, "He has been shot and he is in room 417. Visiting hours start at 11 a.m. until 8 p.m." She hung up. Kerra, who is just observing, said she had to go make rounds and would be back shortly. Then the nurse leaves the room.

Kerra came back in and pulled the curtain around my bed and said, "Why do you call yourself Roarke? Is that for Mr. Roarke?"

"How do you know I call myself Roarke?"

"I heard your phone conversation and the reason I know of Mr. Roarke is because I am a student at Howard

University and the sorority that I was planning to pledge is always saying before you can cross over, Mr. Roarke has to approve you." In my own mind, I thought it was some trick. "So, are you the Mr. Roarke they talk about?"

"Maybe, maybe not."

"I think you are." Then she slobbered my knob – translation: sucked my dick – like there was no tomorrow, saying stuff like, "I really want to get in to that sorority." I am loving this. She is actually doing the catcall and waving sorority signs as she is destroying my knob.

The curtain was pulled back and she does not even notice it. It's my brother, Shake. Man, he was a welcome sight as he pulled the curtain open and said, "Roarke."

She turned around, embarrassed. But, she doesn't stop. I am weak. But, I get her off my knob.

Shake said, "Roarke, I thought this was the wrong room." He came over and hugged me, and then broke down crying.

Pause: My brother Shake is the most thorough man I know. He has whipped many a man's ass for messing with me and almost killed a few dudes for messing with my sisters or mother. So in my own words, Shake was the Mohammed Ali of the hood. He loved five things: his family, his women, his children, his forty-ounce beer, and his Newports.

BTS:

So after Shake got himself together, he said, "Roarke, who was that sucking your joint? She was doing such a good job, my joint got hard. Can she come back and break me off too?"

We are laughing now And I said, "Shake, I love you. Thanks for coming to see me."

"I have been downstairs since 7 a.m. since M called me and told me you were shot. I walked down here. You know I'm always down here. What happened?" I told him. Then he said, "Man, folks go crazy over some pussy. Look at you in the hospital getting serviced." Then Shake said, "Roarke, on the serious side, I have been praying for you and I know M has been laying on her face most likely talking in tongues, doing all that stuff that they were doing in church when I went with you. I prayed from the moment I heard until I finally saw you."

Now, I'm teary eyed.

Let Me Flow

My brother is praying

I am still playing

I thought he was a fool

But I am

He is trying

To change

I am still the same

BTS:

Shake said, "Roarke, our father is downstairs."

I said, "Who?"

"Our father."

"Ronald is downstairs?"

"Yeah. He got here five minutes after me."

"Go get him and send him up."

Reflection:

My father and I have not spoken in years. We were beefing over something that never happened and I despised him because as much as I didn't want to be like him and treat women the way he treated my mother, I actually became him in every way, good and definitely the bad. Even though my brother has his name, I am the one that acted like him. We never called him Daddy. We called him by his first name, Ronald.

BTS:

So he came up to the room and hugged me. He said, "What's up, boy? You alright? Do I need to go kill somebody?" My father is straight hood. He would kill someone and not give it a second thought.

Pause: This is truly where my playa ways come from. This man invented the game. In the encyclopedia, under the word "game," there was a picture of my father—inventor, innovator—along with this definition—to enhance upward mobility of yourself at all times at any cost to control thoughts before they are even thought. That is the meaning of the word GAME.

BTS:

At one time, I was actually known as Lil Game, after my father. But of course, I changed it to Mr. Roarke, which actually means Game. Mr. Roarke controlled the game.

I said, "Ronald no. You do not need to kill anyone. It was all over a stupid girl."

Ronald said, "Who was she?"

"It was not one of my girlfriends. It was some knucklehead's girlfriend, one of my boys."

He got closer to me, shook my hand, and said, "Boy am I glad that you're alright."

"Thanks Ronald."

"I'm still going down to Barry Farms. I don't plan to kill nobody. But, don't nobody shoot my son."

"Ronald, no need to. Let's squash this right here." So, he left the room. I dozed off to sleep for a few hours. Then I woke up because someone was whispering, "Roarke, Roarke." I looked up and did not recognize the voice or the face.

She said, "You don't know my face. But you should recognize my voice since I am the one you always stand up."

I said, "Oh, Nicole?"

She said, "Yes, Roarke, Nicole. How are you? How did you get shot? I only came to see you because I did not believe you."

Then I responded, "Why didn't you believe me?"

She said, "Come on, Roarke. You have stood me up ten times. How could I believe you?"

Then she started to leave. I said, "No Nicole, please don't leave me."

"All of a sudden you've got feelings? You did not think of me all those times you stood me up." Then she walked out the door.

To my surprise, Dré walked in with all the fellas—Reg, Darnell, Tre and everybody we hung with. It must have been about twenty fellas. That really bought my spirits up.

Then Dré said, "Roarke, who was that honey leaving your room? I don't know her."

I said, "Dré, that's that honey that I kept standing up from Silver Hill Road."

Dré said, "Why you stand her up?"

"Come on Dré. When did I have time to do her?"

Then Reg said, "Roarke, I can take her off your hands." All the fellas laughed. Then, she walked back in the door and sat down while the fellas talked and joked about my gunshot wound, sports, and who gets the most pussy. One of the fellas secretly tried to holla at her, which I thought was funny.

Let Me Flow:

The Fellas

Through good and bad

Thick and thin

The fellas are always here

Since we were young

To us all getting older

The fellas are always here

To helping me fix flat tires

To helping me wash my car

The fellas are always here

To this shooting nonsense

The fellas are always here

BTS:

While one of my boys named Joseph is hollering at Nicole, the rest of the fellas stated, "Roarke, you see him hollering at your girl?"

I said, "Yeah I see him and yes he is disrespecting me in his own way. But, fellas, pull up close and let me tell you a secret." They all pull up close. "Remember prom night back in 1985 when he couldn't find Cicely, the girl he has the baby by now?"

They all said, "Yeah."

"The reason he couldn't find her is because when they went to the prom, I picked her up ten minutes after they arrived, took her to the hotel on Bladensburg Road, and tore that pussy up for about two hours. Then, I dropped her off in front of the building where the prom was. She told him she was out front waiting for him. So, he can have Nicole 'cause he still don't know I was his baby's mother's first, not him. She was not a virgin prom night for him. I had already popped that coochie earlier."

All the fellas started laughing.

Joseph said, "What y'all laughing at over there?" No one can even speak at that moment. "Somebody must be saying something funny."

Dré jumped in and said, "Joseph, just keep doing your thing. We're not talking about you." So, he continued to holler at Nicole.

Pause: Fellas, if you don't play your cards right, there is always someone like me that will have your girl. So make sure you play the best hand you have because if you don't, you have left yourself open for someone with real game, like me, to take your woman!

BTS:

Since there were so many people in the room, the nurse came in and asked if most of them would leave so that I could get some rest. I asked Nicole to stay. All the fellas shook my hand and said, "We will be back tomorrow."

Dré said, "Roarke, I will be back later today. I'm going home to get some sleep. I have not slept since you got shot."

I said, "Dré, stay a while longer." So, I introduced him to Nicole and Dré apologized for me, stating it was his fault that I could never keep a date with her. But, he would change that by giving us some quality time today.

He came over, hugged me, and said, "Man, get better soon. I know you don't want to hear this. But, I think we need to start going to church."

I laughed and said, "Dré, I agree."

He then walked out of the hospital room. Nicole sat on the side of the bed and said, "Roarke, I actually like your buddy, Dré. He seems really cool especially about you. You sure y'all not gay?"

Pause: Women I know there is a whole lot of stuff going on now – and there was stuff going on in the 80s and 90s. But, just because a guy has a good best friend that's a male and they spend a lot of time together, does not mean they're gay! Dré and I have known each other since we were in pampers. His mother is my mother and my mother is his mother. So do not judge your man because he has a guy friend that he is always with.

BTS:

So Nicole said, "Roarke, I did not mean to offend you." I told her she didn't. Some people have said that before. Dré and I know who we are. So it does not offend us. If folks actually knew how much pussy we really got, it would really hurt their feelings.

Then I said, "Enough about that. Let's talk about us. Let me state for the record, I plan for my first date outside of this hospital to be with you, wherever you want to go, whatever you want to do."

She said, "First Roarke, let's get to know each other. The only thing we know about each other is where each of us live."

"For real? That's all I want you to know for now. Let's hang out and see where it goes. I think you can learn too much too quick and start judging the other person."

"I disagree. But, I can try something new with you."

As I dozed off to sleep, she pulled up close, kissed my cheek and said, "Get well soon. I will call you." She walked out of my hospital room. In a deep trance, not asleep, but a trance, thoughts run rampant through my head:

Slow down

I am running

Too fast

I am crawling

Scratching

Slow down

Crying and feeling faint

Slow down

Helpless and abandoned

Slow down

Crazy deranged

And helpless

Slow down

Is this the

Part you take

My feelings and step on them

Slow down

I snap out of my trance. I called my mother. She picked up on the fourth ring.

"Hello."

I said, "M, it's me."

"Roarke, you okay?"

"Yeah, but I can't sleep. I need you to pray for me."

She started praying. "Dear Heavenly Father, I come to you on behalf of my youngest son. Heal his body. Heal his soul. But, God, most of all, please heal his whorish ways. In Jesus' name, I pray. Amen, amen, amen." She then said, "Now go to sleep. I love you."

"I love you, too, Mom."

I finally dozed off into Dreamland. Around midnight, I felt heat beside me. I realized it's a body. I looked over and it's the nurse, Akinnesha, lying with me. I was too weak to move so I moved close to her and dozed off.

It's Sunday morning. I don't remember what happened last night. When I woke up, my bed was all wet and my dick was dripping cum. The nurse was still in the room. She rolled me to another bed and gave me a sponge bath mixed with a massage–mixed with her giving me a tongue lashing on my balls, which set me off completely.

Let Me Drift:

A tongue

In the right place

A tongue licking

Oh my goodness

A tongue

Taking care of me

A tongue is dangerous

A tongue is special

A tongue can be a marvelous thang!

BTS:

So she is finishing me off and I am feeling guilty. This is what got me into the hospital, a woman. I think I need to chill. She dries me off and gives me a pair of underwear and a t-shirt. I ask her for her phone number. She writes it down. Then I ask her to leave.

She asks, "Why do I have to leave?"

"My mother will be here today and the doctor said that if my heart rate does not go down and stabilize, he will not let me go home today."

"Your heart rate will stabilize once I am out of the room and you are not aroused anymore." Little did she know, the candy striper, Kerra, also said she would come by and do something special before I left.

My mother and oldest sister came in, then, my two other sisters, my cousin, and then, Shake and Dré. All of the family was here. When the doctor comes in, he takes me out of the room so he can do one last X-ray. All of my family is still in the room.

While I am in the X-ray room, the doctor positioned me where the bullet was and stated, "Take it easy for a few weeks and please chill out from the ladies for a while. It that bullet didn't kill you; those women are going to kill your body. What I did not tell you, young fella, is that your body is older than you are, really."

I said, "Hold up, doc. Break that down for me."

"Here it is in a nutshell. Your sexual activity for all these years has made your body age ten years faster than usual."

"I still don't understand doctor."

"Son, you have bust so many nuts as if you are ten years older. The body was not made to be abused. It's like a drug addict or an alcoholic, you have similar symptoms. But yours are in your lower abdomen, stomach, and back. They have numerous strains in them, which will eventually lead to a strain in the groin. So, young man, slow down."

Let Me Slide:
Another warning
Slow down from a doctor
Stop now in my tracks
It's going to kill me
Another warning
Take it easy
Leave the girls alone
For a while
Another warning

BTS:
He rolls me in a wheelchair back to my room. My family is still there, as well as Kerra. He gives them the thumbs up and Kerra comes over and plants a big kiss on my lips.

My mother cleared her throat. "Excuse you, young lady. You don't even know my son."

Pause: My mother, sisters, and niece are very protective of me where women are concerned. That's exactly why I don't bring them around. I have to be serious about the woman for them to meet my mother and I have to be straight up in love to introduce them to my sisters and niece..

BTS:

My mother grabs Kerra by the hand and asked, "What are your intentions with my son?"

Kerra said, "I just want to have fun for right now with Roarke. I am finishing up my degree at Howard and I am not sure what the future holds for Roarke and I."

Pause: Honesty – women and men, honesty is the biggest turn on even if I don't like what you said or are saying. But, if it's honest, I can do nothing but respect you. I have always been honest with women, which has lead to some terrific pussy that I could not have gotten if I had lied.

BTS:

So, my mother said to her, in a sarcastic manner, "Roarke needs more from a woman than just fun." She elaborates, "He wants to get married, and I want some grandchildren from him soon."

Kerra responded. "I understand Ms. Edwards. But for real, It's Roarke's choice."

The room immediately got quiet. Then, my mother cursed her out. (Man, I could not wait to get out of that hospital.) It's enough drama being shot, but to have my mother curse someone out in the hospital and have the hospital basically throw us all out is kind of embarrassing, even for me!

So, I am at my mother's house relaxing the first day out of the hospital. But I pack my stuff that evening because I have to get from under her roof. After I pack the last of my things, I page Dré. He calls me right back and said, "I will be there in fifteen minutes."

I go to my mother's room and let her know that I will not be staying for the week as originally planned. She got angry and said, "Boy, you don't know what you have in a mother."

"You right. Sometimes I don't," I said under my breath.

Let Me Flow:

Mothers

Always looking for the best

In you

Always trying to make you

Fulfill a Dream

A Dream that was never yours

But also a Dream

That's worth pursuing

A mother

Chastising and praising at the same time

Will do anything for you because

That's a Mother

BTS:

Dré knocks on the basement window. I raise up slowly because I am still in pain from the gunshot wound and I am still on medication. I feel woozy as I walk to open the door.

Dré said, "Roarke, you look terrible."

"Dré, I will look worse if I stay here." I gave Dré my bag and we were out. I was tired of my mother. I loved her. But, as you already know, I was my own man and I always did my own thang, good or bad. I was my own man.

Dré said, "Roarke, do you want to go to my house so you can rest and no one will bother you?"

"No, Dré. Bring me to my condo."

So, he did just that. We get to the towers and there are a few people in the lobby. Dré had my bag on his back.

I told him, "Lets take the freight elevator." I did not want anyone to see me in this condition. So, we went up in the freight elevator. I could not find my keys, so Dré used his set. So I am finally in the house. I ask Dré could he go get my mail. I give him the key out of the candy dish. I put my pajamas on so I can relax and get myself some hot coco.

Pause: Hot coco is my cure for everything. Since I was a child, it has been my cure-all. It always makes me feel better.

BTS:

I am propped up in my bed feeling real comfortable. I have actually started to dose off until I hear footsteps. So I look up. But, I don't see anyone. So, I close my eyes and start to pray. "

Hey God, it's me again. Thanks for everything. From my near death, to having a good family and good friends. In Jesus' name, I pray, amen, amen, amen."

I am sleep. It seems like for days. Then, I feel hands around my neck. I am too weak to fight. Dré must have left the door unlocked. I am loosing my breath fast. My body is weak and since I had been shot, I have not moved my left arm until now. There is a pillow over my face.

Let Me Flow:
Who is this?
Why are they trying to kill me?
What did I do to them?
With my track record
It could be anyone
I sleep with everybody
I have never had a cut card
Or cared for anyone other than myself
I might just deserve to die.

The End

Acknowledgements

I would like to thank God for all His grace and mercy have bought me through. I am living each moment because of you.

"I Love You" is not sufficient for my wife Judy and my two wonderful children, Kayla and Rodney. I ask that God always keep them and keep me humble. Always shout out to Barry Farms--that's where it all started.

Darrell Barnes, Lisa and Keith Tillman, Lil Benny. Troy Ghost Host Rawlings--Troy is my prayer partner, business partner and baddest publicist around. Check him out at www.myspace.com/troyghosthost. Darrell Morrison for hanging out with Taboo Tour- much love and respect. Tia the travel agent- thanks for everything- and for being on front cover. Tyi Flood of www.im4radiodc. com—you helped blow the Taboo tour up. Lamont Carey from "The Wire"-Thanks for having me on your show. www.LacareyEntertainment.com. Keno Davis and the street team. Keesha Parker, Alicia Tutt and Sisters of Unity Book club. Nalo Ervin and all the ladies that met with me at Cheese Cake Factory. To my fellow authors who keep me ready for what ever is next. Candice , Jessica Tilles ,Ronda Rountree, K. Lowery Moore, Saundra Harris, Yasmin Shiraz, King Jewell, Marlene Rickert, DC Bookman and Tiah. The ladies at Urban Knowledge in Mondawmin Mall, Baltimore, MD. Thanks for loving me. J.Tremble/Secrets of a Housewife.

Emily Henry of EmHenry.com- Thanks for all you have done with the tour and just for being a nemesis when I needed. You are terrific.

Kiera Smith, Michelle Donnelly thanks you ladies are the bomb. My barber and friend Dre of Razor Images. Darryl Wade, Kevin Brown and all the barbers at Classic Kutz in SE, D.C. RIP Mr. JACK. My friend and typist Michelle Coles Johnson. Thank you. Vera Kholheim/Ms B/Shannell Davis and Levon, Rhonda and Clyde Duncan. E from market at St. Mary's. My family Marsha, Ruth, Robyn, Rocky, Ronda, Melvin, Kristen, Big Moe, Pete, Brandon and MiMi. Special shout outs to Johnny Whalen Cousin Shay, Delvan Dorsey, Trenell McCauley, Mark , Tonya Frederick –TVF Consulting www.tvfconsulting. com, Sheila Griffin the toy lady, Adult Novelties by Pleasurable Secrets--pleasurablesecrets.sheila@gmail. com 240-604-6503. Lady J and Ms Kris of CWT Radio,

David Thomas , Jimmy Twitty my friend Poetic Derrick, everyone that cam to studio for my show each week. Michelle Carswell of Hair Quarters, Lajuan Barnett- you will always be my biggest fan, Judy's coworkers. Gary Batman Green and Family- thanks for looking out for a brother from the BigCHAIR. Thanks to Renee and Black rocket TV for taping my TV show. To have an exclusive Taboo Talk at your location contact Troy Ghost Host Rawlings 443-740-4285

Book 4, 5 willl be out later this year
www.whatidoistaboo.com